kissing frogs for a while

notionpress.com

kissing frogs for a while

Pavan Tarawade

notionpress.com

Notion Press

Old No. 38, New No. 6,

McNichols Road, Chetpet,

Chennai - 600 031

First Published by Notion Press 2015

ISBN: 978-93-5206-255-3

This book is dedicated to my father
– Vijay Tarawade.

He still owes me the drink he had promised me when I got my first job.

The book is based on a collection of real life incidences involving people I have come across. The names or situations mentioned are, however, purely fictional, and any resemblance should be considered as a coincidence.

Acknowledgements

- Srushti Rao
- Kaustubh Laddha
- Rahul Gaikar
- Hemant Bhardwaj
- Yugmala Singh
- Hardik Patel
- Manish Singh

PREFACE

Greek mythology talks about King Pygmalion of Cyprus, who made a sculpture of a woman and named it Galatea. An artist he was, after all, and spent so much heart on the sculpture that he fell in love with it. He prayed to Goddess Venus, and she bestowed magic over the statue and brought it to life. Pygmalion took great care of her and you know the next part. They lived happily ever after!

Our mythologies depict and preach about stories, wars and love sagas that took place because the Gods and Goddesses blessed or cursed people, as per their whims and fancies. Ever wondered how tough this job must have become for them now, if they did exist in the first place? Cupids are suddenly nowhere to be seen, and there is hardly any talk about soul mates. But love still makes its presence felt subtly in a summer wind that passes by, and in the faces and eyes of beautiful smiling people on the streets. But like beauty, it makes only a transitory appearance these days. Call me old school, but no chatting application beats meeting a person in reality. And no emoticon can ever let you see, how she smiles at you simply through her eyes. This book is, in fact, inspired from such people I have come across; people who did not let their belief wither away in the face of adversity. This book is a dedication to all of them.

Because I think, as we are moving towards getting more and more connected through smart devices and applications, we are moving farther away from one other. Fewer are the number of people who put in an effort to make relationships work. Long distance relationships are started with a tagline saying that they are not meant to work.

I know soul mates aren't anybody's favourite topic to discuss. I am not a big fan either. But I am of the opinion that we seriously don't have a right to play it down, just because we had an unsuccessful relationship or two. I mean, hardly any one of us really goes out of our way looking for the right person. It starts with looking for a good looking person in your junior high classroom, ending it in a year and realizing that it was nothing but a crush, and that maybe, you had a good person in your friend waiting to date you. By the time you come out of these 'not so right' people for you, you are left with no time to search for the right one. And then we give up saying that this is life and crap like that. Most people, who emphasize that they do not believe in love, simply mean that they do not believe so much in people any more.

I tell you what is not correct. Logic! The logic that we seek in an answer to why we even love someone! Because it doesn't have to be logical; it doesn't have to make sense. That is what attracted us to that person in the first place, right? That is what had put a smile on our face - being illogical with her or him. To let our minds run open, naked and childlike stupid in the wide open field, because it was not alone. It was held hand in hand with her or his and looked after. And then we got back to reality, the real people and real life who demanded sense in whatever we did. More sense and less stupid-happiness! And we fell for it, we let go of that hand because it seemed illogical to us now, to run wildly happily and stupidly together. We let it go because it did not fit well into the future others designed for us to live in. We let the only person go, who once let us laugh out without caring how it looked. The one with whom we did not feel shame, did not feel naked. We let the love go. Honestly, if we are not willing to sound stupid, then maybe we don't deserve to be in love. Then those tears we may shed won't make any sense.

Soul mates exist or maybe they don't. But I can guarantee you that there are a few people worth searching for. So shake up your heart a bit. Take it out for a walk. Its wounds were healed a long time back. Let it breathe again and look for someone with a rhyming beat.

Ayesha certainly believes that. So come on! Let's hear her out!

Chapter 1

Somewhere in Andheri West, Mumbai
A flat on the second floor
Ayesha's room

"The first time I saw you at Mehta Uncle's place, I had fallen for you. Miss Sakshi. Will you marry me?" says a guy in a black Raymond suit as he pops open the ring box, as he goes down on one knee, and looks dramatically into an overdressed girl's eyes. The girl then responds with artificial tears at the perfect time and nods. 'Diamonds Are Forever' - the clichéd line follows at the end of the commercial."

"Bravo! Awesome! Who the f*** does that? Where the hell do you find such guys, huh?" Ayesha exclaimed, clearly not impressed by the TV commercial. She then looked at her mother for her reaction.

"Well, first of all, stop saying the 'F' word. okay? And yes, people do it, sweetie! Your father did!" her mom answered with a perfect smile. "Yes, maybe not in such a dramatic fashion wearing a black suit or something, but I remember perfectly how he had gone down on one knee and asked me to marry him." Her eyebrows rose dramatically and fell down as she said that.

"Wow, you were one lucky chick, mom. Must have been crazy! And you said yes?" Ayesha asked, making her eyes large before she corrected herself. "Oh sorry, what a stupid question! Of course you did. That's how I happened. Hehehe!" they both giggled.

"Yes, I said yes, and he knew my answer already. I mean we were at the Railway station when he asked me to marry him. We were waiting to hop into any train that would come in the next five minutes. So, you know I thought it was better to say yes since I had run away from home with this handsome looking guy," laughingly her mom continued the story.

"Yes, absolutely the right thing to do, mother! I wish I were that lucky." Ayesha spoke looking out of the window next to her bed. The December breeze moved a few strands of hair on her face away and the moonlight crawled inside the room.

"Hmm. So what about Piyush? Does he ever call you? Is he seeing anyone?" suddenly the smile disappeared from Ayesha's face, as well as that of her mother's.

"No more Piyush, mom. I told you. We are done. It has been a year and half since we broke up. He is probably chasing some girls out there in Germany. Why do I even care? We broke up. Just don't ask me about him." Ayesha's voice moved rhythmically up and down as she blurted out the words.

"Okay, I won't, sweetie. I don't want to hurt you. But I just do not understand this break up thing you youngsters keep talking about. 'Break up'! Somebody comes up with this term, and every guy and girl of your age just starts using it randomly. A fight or two over silly things and they say, 'We broke up.' How convenient is that for some people!

It just saves the effort of saving a relationship between two people, who say first that they are crazy about each other. Break up!"

"Mom, look here!" Ayesha wrapped her arms around her mother and said gently, "Look at me. I am good, okay. I'm doing great. Yes, I admit, I used to miss him. I used to miss him like crazy earlier, but now I'm kind of getting used to the whole thing. And he was…well, sorry for the word, but he was, and is, an asshole. So, I'm happy that I am not with him. So, stop worrying about your daughter. She is going to find a nice guy."

Her mother smiled and Ayesha raised her eyebrows. She tried to imitate her mom's voice while speaking, *"Ayesha, you are 28 now. You have to get married soon. Why don't we ask Ishaan Uncle if he knows some good guys? What about your friends? You don't like anyone? Naveen. I like Naveen. Such a sweetheart he is! And you have known him for so long. Why don't you marry him? He always liked you. What is the trouble?"*

Pushing away Ayesha's arms from around her, her mother said, "See, you are still not taking it seriously. Otherwise we will have to get you registered onto one those matrimony websites. You decide."

"Uhh! For God's sake, not matrimony websites, mom!" Ayesha shrugged her shoulders and raised the volume of the television set again.

Ayesha's mother had got married when she was 22. Ayesha's father was 24 at that time. She had still not forgotten the day they both ran away from their house in Ahmadabad. It was the early monsoons of 1983, and he had booked tickets in three trains, thinking they might miss one or two.

"Did dad also propose to three women, thinking one or two might say No?" Ayesha had her witty reply ready for her mother.

Ayesha's mother knew that they had not given her any siblings, and nor did Ayesha have many friends. Rocky, her dog, and Naveen were the only two good friends she had. So Ayesha's father and she always gave Ayesha as much freedom as they could. But when it came to choosing a guy for her, they were pretty clear. Clear as in which guys they did not want!

The first time Ayesha got Piyush home, her mother had seen signs of trouble. She felt that the guy would never settle down. He would always want to keep flitting from one place to another, from one heart to the next one. She called him a butterfly. Ayesha wanted to prove them wrong. And she did get quite lucky, in a way. She would get him home to meet them during festivals, and on every other occasion she could think of. She loved watching him talk about sports and politics with her father. "*You are not going to have a drink with daddy. Not so soon. Otherwise they will think you drink a lot or something. My mother will start with her predictions right away then,*" Ayesha would remind him every time. But secretly she always saw them sharing a drink together on the couch in future.

Ayesha's parents had seen her cousins remaining unmarried in their late thirties, some even divorced. They clearly did not want her to follow suit. Nor did they want her to compromise on her freedom or choose some less deserving guy. They respected her faith in marriage even after her break up with Piyush. Her mother had always been there for her, from attending her first dance performance in school, to supporting her through the break-ups she had had. Ayesha was very close to her for the same reason.

But Ayesha had heard enough about matrimony websites and marriages. She was also tired of people linking her up with Naveen. He was her childhood friend, her best friend. But that is as far as she wanted it to be.

Naveen was one of the good looking guys in J.N.T. College. According to Ayesha, he was the best looking one, as also the one who underestimated himself a lot.

"Ayesha, why don't you go around with Naveen? He is so handsome. I am kind of jealous of you," her female friends would say. "Oh, please, he is my friend. He is my best friend and I cannot think of him like that. Never!" Ayesha would reply.

Apparently Naveen did not share the same notion. He liked Ayesha. All the time! He was not a man who was good when it came to women, despite his good looks. For him the word 'love' would only ring one name – Ayesha, whom he had known since their childhood days. He did confess his feelings to her a couple of times. But she kept saying no. Laughing it off, in fact!

He did like a few other girls in their college. But he was too shy and awkward to make a move. Ayesha always made fun of him over that. She even tried to set him up with a girl named Pooja, whom he had a big crush on. He ended up going up to her, and talking about chemistry notes, as vague words tumbled out of his mouth. Needless to mention, the girl who probably liked him for his looks, was totally disappointed and walked away.

Chapter 2

"Either my Facebook profile has turned into a wedding album, or I am getting really old." Ayesha spoke to her colleague as she browsed through the website during her lunch hour at the office.

"Well, I would say both, honey," the girl said, while casually pushing her cushioned chair out of the small cubicle and stretching her arm towards Ayesha.

"I'm getting married!" she said, handing over an envelope to Ayesha. The envelope was white in colour with a golden embossing on top of it.

Ayesha looked at her in disbelief for a few seconds. The very next moment, she jumped out of her chair to congratulate her.

"Wow! This is great news! The guy from the matrimony website, right? That is good, *yaar*. I never knew those things work."

"Well, it worked for me, fortunately. After spending some time together, we realised that we both wanted similar things in life. It is not bad, you know, it is almost the same like you are getting set up by your friends. I mean, you can try that too. I am just saying," she said sympathetically to Aycsha.

"Well, let's see. I have not really given it a thought," Ayesha said with a false air of coolness. Smiling a little, she got back to her cabin.

Despite not wanting to do so, her first thought flew to Piyush. Her hands held the phone even before she thought of it.

She then kept it back and typed in the words – 'Piyush' in the search bar of her Facebook profile. She had deleted him from her friend list a long time back. She did that because she could not bear to see him with random European girls, arms around them and 'smiling' - A thing she couldn't do for a long time without having him by her side.

She went to his profile. It was not the first time she was 'stalking' him on Facebook. His cover picture showed him sitting outside some restaurant with a bunch of people.

"*Maybe he is dating that Indian girl on his right, or maybe he is with the blonde one on the other side,*" she thought to herself, before logging out, and picking up the file on the desk to divert her attention. An attempt made in vain!

That evening the way to her home felt even lonelier, even farther than every other day, as thoughts of getting married now lingered in her head.

She kept thinking about her best friends getting married, the ones who were already engaged and the few others who had chosen to be in a live in relationship; for they could not commit their future to someone they had been seeing for years.

She was getting restless, missing and hating Piyush even more than before.

By the time she had reached home, her eyelashes were wet with tears. She wiped them off, trying not to let her parents get an inkling of it.

She stormed straight to her room and let out the gush of tears waiting to burst out on her pillow.

Time was slipping away. She suddenly felt much older now, felt the urgent need to decide upon the things she had been procrastinating over for so long.

Days had turned into months and months into years, but these still seemed like seconds whenever she thought of Piyush.

"Is he really seeing someone? When is he planning to get married? To whom? Shall I call him once just to see if he is at all interested in..?. What am I even thinking?" Ayesha cursed her own mind for thinking about him yet again. She thought of calling Nisha, the only common friend she had had with Piyush. More because she wanted to know what was happening in his life. She did not recall the last time she had spoken to Nisha. During the time when she dated Piyush, she always considered Nisha a problem. In fact, she even fought with him a couple of times, since she believed Nisha had a huge crush on him. She had warned him that Nisha was super-jealous of their relationship.

Contrary to that, Nisha had recently tied the knot with her long time boyfriend, Amit.

Ayesha thought for a minute before dialling Nisha's number on her phone.

It kept ringing. "Maybe they are busy making out or something," came a weird thought to Ayesha's mind, and she kept the phone down before replacing it with the TV remote control.

She thought of the times when she used to talk for hours with Piyush every night. She remembered when once Piyush had to give a supposedly important presentation at his University in Germany to present his thesis. Ayesha never once forgot to wish him on such occasions. She did not that night either. She called him and heard the phone play its complete ringtone. She kept calling him, but there was no response. She was furious. She wanted to tell him that this was the reason why she kept on doubting him.

But then eventually she had put the phone away and tucked herself in bed. The thought of him flying to India soon put a smile on her face. He was coming for her birthday, and to spend time with his parents. That was going to be lovely. Also she knew that Piyush had never once cheated on her. Not even once. Not so far.

Thousands of miles away in Berlin that particular night, Piyush was sipping his fourth glass of whiskey when he heard a knock on the door. He hoped it wasn't Kim, because it was time for Ayesha's phone-call.

It was Kim.

Kim – his lab partner and also a Literature committee member. And it didn't end there. She was also a big fan of his writing. Or that is what she always told him.

"May I join you?"

"Hey, c'mon in. Have a seat," Piyush said. He had got to know Kim while working late in the laboratory one day. She had come to collect the bag she had left behind, and stopped by to check on this cute Indian scientist. Kim was Scottish by birth. They both found comfort in the fact that they did not need to converse in German. English brought them closer and so did Piyush's poetry.

"Thanks," Kim said as he handed over a drink to her. She took off her gloves and held the glass half filled with golden whiskey swaying on top of ice cubes.

"Cheers!"

"So, why were you so upset today? Everything good?" She asked him and zipped open her winter coat to keep it aside.

"Yeah, am alright. Just having some issues back home!" Piyush said, without looking at Kim. He never once shared his relationship troubles with anyone. "Fights are to be sorted out by us not other people," he would tell Ayesha.

"Hey, come here, sweetie. It will be fine," Kim said slowly rubbing his arm.

Piyush looked at her and smiled. It was followed by more comforting words and several refills of whiskey in their glasses. Kim spoke of literature, English football and all the things she knew would make Piyush smile. He compared her with Ayesha in his head, and then resented that thought the very next moment. Yet he felt, she was better in some ways. No possessiveness, no fights, only intelligent witty conversations, and literary talk. And her eyes! Kim had really pretty eyes. The look in her eyes was warmer than the alcohol conquering his senses one minute after another. He put his arm around her and she curled herself, putting her head over his chest. The whiskey bottle knew already that it was going to be blamed the next morning.

Kim turned towards him and looked up to kiss his chin. He put the glass away and stroked her hair gingerly. They did not need words anymore. He closed his eyes as he kissed her lips, as if closed eyes would amend his sins. They struggled to fit on the couch as he unbuttoned her shirt, and she moved her golden hair behind. She dug her nails more into his naked back as he kissed her neck. They breathed heavily now, and their hands rushed to possess what eyes could only dream of otherwise. Wet bodies rubbed against each others, with dews of sweat evaporating off their skin. The cold December night surrendered against the heated two, as they made love on his couch all night long.

The whiskey bottle felt sorry for itself, and for Piyush's phone flashing "Ayesha calling" on its screen several times.

Chapter 3

It is time

"Ayesha, you remember that guy, Sanjeev? The one whom your dear cousin married after going against her entire family, and then divorced a year later?" Ayesha's mother asked her, adjusting her spectacles. And as she did that, she moved the newspaper away from her eyes, to make it more comfortable to read.

"Yup. What about him?" Ayesha asked, while carefully taking a small sip of her first coffee for the day.

"He has already found some new girl and they got married last Sunday. Seema was telling me."

"What are you hinting at, Mother?" Ayesha skipped a few unnecessary dialogues in between and asked.

"I am just saying that it is high time you looked for the right partner to get married to. You know how supportive Papa and I have been. We do not care about caste or whatever. Just find the guy soon. You know you are already…!"

"28!" Ayesha completed her sentence. "Yes, Mom, I know my age and I will do something about it. It is not that easy. There are ten thousand things to look at. I have so much work pressure. That new Boss of ours has added two more supplements to our newspaper and as usual, it is my responsibility to look after those. Okay, anyway, I have to rush now. Tata. Bye bye!" Ayesha hurriedly took the last sip of her coffee and once again diverted her mother's attention elsewhere like the fictitious character, *Vikram* from the *Vikram & Vetaal* tales.

Coming downstairs in a matter of minutes, she unlocked the car. With one foot pressed over the clutch, and the other slightly kissing the accelerator and with the seat belt put on, she turned the car keys. The car roared softly in reply and royally strolled out of the parking lot.

Glancing at herself in the overhead mirror once, she moved the car onto the main road and towards the direction of her office.

Today she was not thinking about how nothing could be done about the slow moving traffic, or why no one ever said anything about the irritating hoardings of politicians at every corner of the city blocking the view ahead. Neither was she occasionally looking at her Sony Experia sitting on the seat next to her to see if it was blinking or not. This everyday routine was replaced by the thought of how the 'marriage thing' could no longer be postponed.

Her whole life was being played like a kaleidoscope of memories before her eyes.

Her friends and she talking about getting married back in school, and how exciting they thought it was, her cousins and her friends who had got married recently, the romantic moments that she and Piyush had shared, the times when they spoke of getting married, their fights, all those mushy Hollywood movies about weddings, white gowns, the aisle, the wedding hall, her colleague talking about matrimony websites…and so many more things.

The sight of 'The Daily Chronicle' in front woke her up from her thoughts. She slowly and cautiously turned the steering wheel. The darkness of the underground parking lot gave her time to wipe the sadness off her face.

Twice making sure that the car was locked with the beeping sound that followed, she marched towards an elevator which took her to her office.

As soon as she entered, the newly appointed receptionist rose from her counter, and spoke with as much respect as she could, "Ayesha Madam, Gulati sir has called you to his cabin. He told me to… I mean he said when you come to tell you, Madam."

Ayesha put a friendly hand over her shoulder and made her sit before saying, "I'll go, alright. And you are doing a good job!"

Ayesha put her bag on the cushioned chair that revolved as soon as the bag fell on it. After greeting a few friendly as well as not so friendly colleagues next to her cabin, she switched on the computer. She made sure there were no assignments pending and reread the ones finished. She tied her hair in a ponytail and moved to Mr Gulati's cabin. He was the Chief Editor of The Daily Chronicle.

"Come in, Ayesha," he beckoned her in even before she could knock.

"Good morning, Sir. You wanted to see me?" Ayesha spoke.

"Morning! Yes, I did. Come in, take a seat." The man in his sixties, but looking much younger, said. He slightly tilted his head to make it visible from the wide screen monitor in front of him as he spoke.

"Ayesha, I am sure you are aware that we have added two new supplements to our paper. Apart from that, we are also thinking of starting a Lifestyle magazine which will target Non residential Indians settled abroad as well as out here. Ayesha, there is going to be a lot more work coming in, and it is a giant leap for this small time newspaper, or let me correct it – 'once used to be –small time newspaper' "Mr Gulati cleared his throat. A sense of pride gleamed in his eyes.

"But that is not why I called you here today," he said and paused for a second. "We have decided to promote you to the Senior Editor's position. The magazine will be yours to take care of. How you want to promote it, what you want to focus on, everything will be yours to decide. Our media group will be coordinating with you for the same. How does that sound to you?" he asked her. He then stretched his arm to give her a few pages of a document to look at.

"That is…it sounds good to me, Sir. Thank you so much for putting your faith in my work and for the opportunity." Ayesha spoke everything that came to her mind.

"You deserve it, Ayesha. We have seen you working so hard since the time you joined Daily Chronicle. And it's a rare talent in you that we do not want to miss. Otherwise your generation is simply busy hopping from one job to another, thinking that is what a career is. But you are special. Good luck, child. Do well!" He said with a fixed smile on his face as Ayesha thanked him politely, and walked out of his cabin.

'Senior Editor'. She had dreamt of this since her college days. Being laughed at by people who felt it was nothing but a dream, being supported by her mother, Piyush, Naveen and a few other close friends.

It was crazy, as it seemed. All of us have some goals, some dreams. Most of us are dreamers. Some of us see these dreams in soft sunlight or a rainy day or in the red fire of a long winter evening. Some of us chase these dreams until we can catch them, while some opt to help others to pursue theirs. Some of us let their dreams die, but others nourish and protect them. Ayesha was among the latter ones. Today she saw her dream come true.

But it was not as she thought it would be. There was no jumping in the air in excitement. No cries of 'wooh'! There were no tears of joy. The friends and people that she often talked to about her dream were not even around. There was just satisfaction. A light feeling inside that it had finally happened!

Maybe because her head was still dominated by the thought of having to get married soon, it murdered the joy of her promotion. She felt and decided that she should be happy. She wanted to celebrate.

She finished her work early and planned that she would leave early from office that day.

"Hello, Naveen! Hey, what's up!" she spoke on her phone in a soft voice, making sure that it wouldn't penetrate the glass door.

"Hey, Ayesha! Hi there. Tell me, how come at this time?" he replied.

"Leave all that. Tell me fast, are you free today? I want to go out somewhere."

"Yeah, I am. But tell me what happened. Anything special? Where do you want to go?"

"Oh, Naveen. Don't ask any questions! Just meet me outside my office at around six. Okay?" she demanded.

"Okay. I will be there. See you then," Naveen spoke without any disagreement.

"Cool. See you!" Ayesha spoke with a little bit of excitement finally, as she disconnected the phone.

"Hey! Guess what?" Ayesha spoke hurriedly as soon as she saw Naveen stepping towards her.

"What? What happened? It is not your birthday. It is not Uncle or Auntie's birthday either. Tell me," said Naveen, who had put on a newly bought *Pepe Jeans* shirt for the special occasion that he did not know anything about. She smiled and hugged him sideways.

"Oh, and your fashion sense is improving. I like the shirt," Ayesha said, and before he could thank her for the same, she continued speaking, "I got promoted! As Senior Editor."

"Nice. Congratulations, *yaar,*" Naveen said, taking his sunglasses off.

"Thanks. Thanks. Now let's go and have some good food somewhere. You don't know what all is happening.

I have to tell you so much. We will take your car for now. Mine is in the parking inside." As she spoke, both of them had already moved towards his Honda City as she usually decided things.

On the way to '*La pizzaria*', the Italian restaurant, she narrated to him the entire episode of her being called to the cabin and Naveen listened to her carefully like a good boy. She even called her parents. She gave them the news of her promotion along with her coming home late that night. They did not have a problem since it was Naveen whom she was with.

Naveen's friends and his parents had often looked at and wished that Ayesha and Naveen could be a couple one day. To be honest, even Ayesha's parents did. Well actually everyone, except Ayesha did.

So here they sat at the table near the corner, after Ayesha changed a couple of tables saying she did not like the view. Naveen asked her what she was planning to do next.

"I'm planning to get married. How is that?" She looked at him, making her eyes big.

"Really?" he said, taking a pause, and then continued. "Yeah, well…even my parents have been asking me the same. What did Uncle and Aunty say?"

"Mom has been driving me crazy. Well, it is not her fault either. I do have to someday. But urrghh, I hate even the thought of it now. I mean where am I going to find the right guy all of a sudden, seriously? Tell me!" she asked him animatedly.

"Well, yes, I know," said the poor chap, who did not take that as an insult. k. He had long back accepted his status of 'one of the million nice guys friend-zoned for a lifetime'.

"Why am I going to put my name up on some matrimony website or something now?" she spoke with anger, as the waiter with the order almost took a step back, wondering if he should come back later.

"Please serve," she told him quietly.

Naveen let the waiter go, and holding a fork and a knife in his hand, he said to Ayesha, "Why not?" Naveen's face now looked blurry through the strong vapours coming off the sizzler on his plate.

"Why not, what?" she almost stopped taking a bite of the French fries stuck to her fork.

"Matrimony websites. That is not such a bad idea, I mean. A lot of people are doing it these days. Good people. People like us, you know. You remember Jason? He did get married through that."

"Jason was crazy anyway, you know that."

"Okay, forget him. What about Snehal? She got married to a guy through a matrimony website," Naveen continued.

"What? What are you saying? And what a bitch! She did not even invite me for her wedding!" Ayesha took the anger out on a piece of already dead chicken with the knife in her hand.

"Well, you stole her last boyfriend. Didn't you?" Naveen laughed out loud.

"Excuse me. Piyush was not her boyfriend. She just had dinner with him twice. That doesn't make someone your boyfriend."

"All right. Let that be. What I am saying is, what is the harm in giving it a try? You can always put the criteria clearly as to what you are looking for, and you know, just filter out guys whom you do not even want to meet." For the first time Naveen dominated a part of the conversation and felt victorious.

"Whatever! Let's see. Today is not the day for that. C'mon, I got my promotion today. And I called you to take me out so that I can divert my mind off stupid things. Mister, you are not doing a good job, you see?" she said with a smile.

"Okay, okay. Agree. Let's go and have some ice cream from *Naturals* after this. Cool?" he said and she agreed to it.

On her way back home, she felt relieved. She did not thank him verbally for always being there as a support, but the goodbye hug said it all.

"Don't think much. Just go home now," he said. "And congratulations, once again! I am really proud of you!"

She waved to him and ran upstairs. Rocky was wagging his tail from the top row of the stairs, looking at her.

At home, her parents knew not to mention the topic of marriage at least for tonight. Instead they offered her a big hug and congratulated her on her achievement. They really were proud of their daughter, and yet secretly worried inside as to how she would find the right guy for herself.

Chapter 4

I think the best form of attraction is between two friends, an attraction which is often left unsaid. You do not meet like lovers the first time. And then, you tell your head, "This is how it is going to be ahead." Friends, Best Friends, Buddies…anything but Lovers! The heart, on the other hand, secretly tucks in a thousand precious connections it feels between the two souls.

Thus, we carry on with our lives. Growing up together, watching each other walk with, run after, fall for, fall out of, and feel happy and sad for others around. Naveen and Ayesha did too. They had known each other from school. Their families knew each other quite well too. So they became friends. However, love likes to grow where it is difficult, where the heart requires rebelling against at least a few, where situations arise when the two need to fight against the odds.

Naveen's parents were especially fond of Ayesha. His sister adored her too. She took every opportunity to paint Piyush as evil in front of Ayesha. Not Naveen! Naveen had always liked Piyush. He knew Piyush was not the barrier that stopped Ayesha from loving him back. It was Ayesha herself. She was not looking for someone like Naveen.

Naveen had confessed his feelings to Ayesha three times in a course of fifteen years. The first time was, when they were in the seventh grade and out on a school trip.

"Ayesha, I want you to be only *my* friend!" he said to her.

Ayesha, wearing her knee length school uniform and a pink ribbon in her hair, started laughing. She did understand what he meant. But she could not be only *his* friend. She had a crush on their school's top basketball player, Sushant. It is a different story that the crush ended not more than five days after the trip. But Naveen had to just sit there and watch her be friends with the tallest guy in their class.

'I want to learn to play Basketball," he had told his mother the next day.

The second time he opened his heart for her was on Christmas in 2005. This time two things were to be blamed. A movie that he had watched – 'A lot like love', and his friend, Aadil, who had told him that even Ayesha liked him back!

Like every Christmas, Naveen was invited over for cake and wine by Ayesha's Catholic mother and her-not-so religious father. The four of them had scrumptious food and sipped on Merlot. Ayesha's father spoke to Naveen about the latest bottle making it to his collection of wines and Naveen simply said, "Wow!" He did not drink anyway. Ayesha, on the other hand, was busy staring at the Christmas tree she had decorated when Naveen walked up to her. "Let's go down for a walk," he 'told' her instead of 'asking' this time. And that worked.

Naveen and Ayesha strolled around her house along the moonlight kissed pathway. Mild winters were kissing her cheeks as Ayesha thought of the year gone by. Naveen, on the other hand, thought of a hundred different ways Ayesha might say 'No', and then smiled at the one way she might say 'Yes' as well.

"Ayesha, I like you. I still do," he said, looking at her.

"I know you do!" came the reply he had not expected.

"Umm…So…you do too?"

"Naveen, I do like you, but you know it is not in the same way. Plus you know I broke up with Shahid just a few months back."

"Oh, okay. You need time? I'm sorry I know it might be too early. I can wait if you want me to." Naveen tried not to lose his composure.

"You have waited long enough, my sweet friend. That wait is not worth it." She pulled his cheek.

"Naveen, you can get better girls than me. Trust me, champ. Plus let us be what we are, right? We are best at being friends. I cannot see us like that, Naveen. I cannot."

"Okay, alright!" Naveen said, not looking at her this time.

That night the little boy inside Naveen knew for sure that Santa Claus was not real. Because over the years, there had been just one thing on his Christmas wish-list so far!

And the third time when he asked Ayesha out?

Well, let me take you guys to that story a little later.

CHAPTER 5

Ayesha was turning twenty nine in a month's time. The pressure was at its peak. Not from her parents, but in her own head.

She had been a girl who had always believed in marriages, and by marriages I mean love marriages. She did not want to give up on her dream of finding the right guy.

But the truth was that, after her bitter break up with Piyush, she had thrown herself into her job. She had looked after several projects, gone through training and development, taken up leadership roles and built a strong career for herself. And the tougher part which she had survived so far was ignoring the random guys, trying not to fall into a rebound, and enduring the constant mocking from friends and relatives over her being single at this age. And she had tried her best to get over Piyush.

The four and half years that Piyush spent with Ayesha were the best days of his life too. Yes, you heard me. Piyush did make mistakes. He lied. He hurt her feelings. But he loved her more than anything when he was around. She was the first thought on his half sleepy, half awake mind. He hardly ever slept before putting her to sleep. Too much love, in fact! So what did go wrong?

Well, if you look at Piyush's past, Ayesha was the first girl he had fallen in love with, and surely the last one as well. Back in school, he had dated the prettiest of girls. That followed in college as well. Born a poet, words came easy to him, and he knew only too well how to play around with them.

"I was not flirting with her. I only meant to tell her that she was looking good, in a good sense," he would have to calm Angry Ayesha down then.

He used to then take her to their favourite place that offered the best sizzlers in town. There he would have two sided conversations, wherein he would speak first and then imitate Ayesha in her voice. He would try to play with his hair like she did when she talked. Her bubble of jealousy would then burst, and she would hug him tight.

But now she felt like her ship was drowning slowly, with the pressure mounting with every single day that passed. So she shrugged off the pride and some wisdom as well, when she decided to meet a few guys set up by her friends and her nosy relatives. The meetings had turned into fiascos. She was probably not ready, and neither were the guys she was looking for.

So one day, her mom gathered enough guts to ask her that question, "Ayesha sweetie, have you ever given a thought to…matrimony websites?"

Ayesha took a minute to answer it. No longer was she the same old Ayesha who would have exclaimed in disagreement and pushed that possibility out of the window.

"I have, mother. Maybe I will. I guess I will. What's the harm in trying, right? Several of my friends have tried it. And some of them did come across nice guys. I mean that's what they told me," Ayesha spoke without lifting her head up.

Her mother came close to her and said comfortingly, "*Beta*, no pressure, okay? We will just see if we can find some good guys and then decide further. You know, Papa and I have never forced you into doing anything you did not want to. Have we? We do not even mind you waiting for a little longer, if you wish to. Because we ourselves do not want you to end up with someone who does not deserve our sweet daughter. Is that fine?"

"Thanks, mom" Ayesha said kissing her mother's hand.

"We can start right away. What say?" she said and both of them moved to her bedroom and her laptop.

We all share some or the other opinion about matrimonial websites. Possibly each one of us has been annoyed at least once, with emails floating in from matrimonial sites spamming our inbox. Most of us have also been greeted by pop up screens that break through our antivirus programs, displaying pictures of good looking men and women, inviting us to join their matrimony portal.

Interestingly it all started around the time when the entire young generation, which had only recently become addicted to online chatting and dating websites, was slowly losing its faith in arranged marriages. Arranged marriages - a concept that can be termed almost sacred when it comes to our religions, societal values and their expectations! Then came a few visionaries who tossed this whole concept of arranged marriages up, moulded it a bit, draped it into a fresh avatar and presented in front of us – matrimony websites!

A lot of people did embrace it happily and are now happily (?) married.

So anyway, Ayesha and her mom logged into one such website.

'LetsGetMarried.com'

"Are you sure this is a good one?" her mother asked, looking at the jazzy design on the welcome screen that opened.

"Well, I'm sure all websites are the same. This is the same one which a few of my colleagues had registered on."

"Oh, god, now I have to go through the painful process of putting in my information!" Ayesha said, thumping the desk in irritation.

"Right! And when you people create those accounts on a new social networking website every month, very happily you fill in all the information. In fact, more than necessary at times," her mother was spot on.

As Ayesha scrolled down the page, she could see that it had a lot more information to be entered than they both had thought.

"Oh, mother, look at these good looking plastic women on the side. So artificial they are! I'm sure they are still unmarried."

"Okay, you pay attention to your thing first, Ayesha. What is this 'caste' thing that they are asking for?" Her mother moved her spectacles little bit closer to her eyes as if that would make a difference.

There was a tab listing hundreds of castes to choose from, along with sub castes if those were not enough.

"Interesting way to endorse caste based discrimination, isn't it? Already people are sick enough to be so caste oriented even today. And then, such things will never give a supporting hand to inter caste marriages. Something which people are fortunately going in for lately!" Ayesha's eyes had no room for mercy.

"Well, they are a website and into business. If they do not provide this option, some other website will, and people will resort to that one. Simple, they are just being professional."

"Oh, mother, I hate it when you are right. But it sucks anyway."

"I know," her mother said. She then asked Ayesha to pause for a minute on the tab of religion which Ayesha had kept unchecked.

"Wait a second, Ayesha, just make sure you don't get a guy from 'that' religion."

"Mom? Seriously? C'mon, not all of them are, you know…!" Ayesha was surprised.

"Well, I know. I'm not illiterate. Those are just a few crazy ones," Her mother said before continuing,

"It is just that, you know…it is just that they smell. They have some weird smell coming from them."

"Hahahhahahah! Mom, you are so hilarious. Where do you get that from?" Ayesha could not stop laughing.

"Okay, as you say. But I do beg to differ." Ayesha continued filling in her information as they both laughed.

The next column said 'Looking for' and displayed a few sample answers for assistance.

"Hmm…This one is difficult. How can I summarise what exactly I'm looking for?" Ayesha bit her lower lip and thought for a minute.

"They should rather ask who I am not looking for. That would be simple, wouldn't it be? Because I am not looking for an asshole or a jerk or a pretentious idiot or someone who wears sharp pointed formal shoes, for someone who looks at one's eyes and not elsewhere while he talks, someone who doesn't lie, doesn't cheat, someone who is not a smoker or a drug addict, someone who is not…!"

"A guy?" her mother interrupted Ayesha finally. "Has my daughter turned lesbian or something?"

"Hehe! Good one, mom. Well, fortunately I haven't. Not yet. Okay, what I am looking for? I am looking for Mr. Darcy, Prince Charming. Can you guys get me that?" she said mocking 'Let's get married.com'.

"Okay, I am leaving if you don't finish up this now. Fill in things properly, *beta*. I guess this is the most important part."

"Alright, alright, I will," replied Ayesha and after some deep thought, knowingly or unknowingly put in the description of Piyush in that box.

After clicking the submit button, they both gave out a sigh of relief.

'Let's get married.com' then opened a new screen which congratulated Ayesha on making the wise decision of registering with them. It showed a list of a few successful couples who had benefited from doing the same at one point of time, and who were now happily married.

"Oh, I do hope so!" said Ayesha with a mixture of sarcasm and hope.

Next they checked a few profiles of men registered on the website.

The first one displayed a picture of a guy in formal attire with the tie almost suffocating him around his neck. Ayesha wondered if he would be using the same photograph on his job resume.

It said, 'Looking for – A girl who is well educated, fair, (slightly dark will also do), of medium height and weight, watches cricket and cooks food'.

"Wow , wake up to reality, men! This is for a life partner hunt, not a fairy out of your tale."

The second profile had a picture of a guy with a big broad smile on his face. Clearly he must have been asked by his parents to do so.

Since his 'Looking for' column said – 'Looking for a girl for our son who is working but is very traditional. She must be well trained in handling domestic responsibilities. The one who prefers traditional attire to the western one will be preferred.'

"Impressive!" said Ayesha clapping her hands. "I am pretty sure in future he'll be asking his mother permission for whether he should sleep with his wife on a particular day or not!"

A few of the profiles even included a video message where the guy seemed more desperate than a salesman, moving from door to door to sell encyclopaedia.

Ayesha and her mom agreed to the fact that the online matrimony had really become a big industry when they saw several categories such as weddings for elite, assisted marriages, where a dedicated manager would tailor search profiles based on one's expectations. They even came across a few specialized matrimony mobile applications which, once downloaded on your phone, would let you chat with other registered users and take it further.

"Mom, it's better if we look into these profiles later. I cannot read all this right now. Not right now," Ayesha said before closing the website window and shutting down the computer.

"Mom?" She said before resting her head on her mother's lap.

"Yes, sweetie?" her mother slowly caressed her hair while taking her glasses off.

"I'll get the right guy I'm looking for, no?"

"Yes, you will, my child. Don't worry. Let's be patient and hopeful with this, okay?" Her mother was happy that she found the right words to comfort her daughter.

Ayesha slowly closed her eyes and tried to take a small nap on her mother's lap. The last time she did that was almost two years back when she had broken up with Piyush.

Both she and her mother pretended not recalling that.

Chapter 6

The memories that remain…

Time heals all the wounds. Does it? Or is it the maturity that we gain over time that helps us understand the things we need to let go of and the things that are worth holding onto?

Ayesha was looking at the star-studded sky through her bedroom window. The moon looked so picture-perfect tonight. She suddenly felt an urge to tell someone so. The next moment she just let it go. Clearly the moon has been an object of inspiration and admiration for millions of poets and lovers over thousands of years. But for Ayesha, the moon was something that did not let people get over each other. She felt it was a doorway to nostalgia. She felt it was mocking her with a smirk on its face.

She diverted her eyes from that pitiless moon and turned back inside. But the moon had already played its trick. Her mind was now time-travelling into the past, taking her to him again, to their bitter sweet memories and all the times that they had laughed together, hugged and kissed. She touched the fingertips of her one hand with the other, trying to feel the warmth of his hand that she missed so much now. She thought of the first time ever when they had kissed, and how she would feel protected from the world with his wide arms around her. She missed listening to the beat of his racing heart that she would rest her head on. Even the cold December breeze that entered through the window and gently flirted with her hair was acting melancholy to his voice. She smiled as she remembered his eyes at one moment, and felt increasingly jealous and hurt at the thought of another woman being in his arms.

Piyush!

A science graduate and an aspiring scientist! The first guy that Ayesha had ever fallen in love with so hopelessly, and the one she had trouble getting over with.

He was six feet tall with an athletic physique and dark brown wavy hair resting on his forehead. Although he was a science student, he would secretly indulge in writing poetry whenever he got time. Words and a crackling sense of humour were his best weapons. The weapons Ayesha did not have a defence against, and instead chose to melt into.

Tirelessly he would tell Ayesha, every now and then, how beautiful she was and how her specs and her sharp eyes tuned him on. "You make me feel I should quit my age old passion of becoming a Nobel Prize winning scientist one day for decoding a sequence responsible for lipase activating hormones in yeast *sacharromyces cerevisiae* ,and instead become a poet for life," he would tell her, holding her chin in his left hand. She would just smile in reply and hug him tight. She would then struggle to raise her toes to rest her head over his shoulder.

It was never anything but love between them. The first day she saw him coming out of that parking lot, Piyush had come up to her and asked her for her number. And she did give it, much to Naveen's surprise, to a very random stranger for the first time. She did not regret it as they met at a pizza place the following weekend, followed by a movie and had had their first kiss already by the beginning of the third week.

It was then he told her that he was going crazy about her and could not stop thinking about her even for a micro second. She had her eyes still closed from their first kiss, and simply smiled in reply, before putting her arms around his neck and kissing him gingerly, while whispering, "I think I'm more than crazy about you. And I think I can keep kissing your lips till eternity."

He took her out to a dining place in the outskirts of the city when she had got her first job as a newspaper reporter. Looking at the faint candle light flicker over his face, she knew already it was he whom she wanted to share the rest of her smiles with.

Smiles, tears, hugs, fights and kisses - they shared it all over the next few years. A lot had changed. Once an independent girl, she was now sort of dependant on waking up to his poetic words waiting in her inbox, to his surprising her with a single gerbera in his left hand at her office, while picking her up and putting her to sleep every time she had a bad day at work.

And then there came a clichéd, yet unavoidable stage of life. The stage where you realised that it was not a fairytale, and that you might have to part from each other for a while, be it for career or something else.

"Why do you have to go abroad? Can't you stay back here?" she kept asking him, every now and then, although knowing secretly the answer was no. Piyush gave out a sigh indicating his irritation over answering the same question and convincing her yet again.

"Ayesha, I have worked my ass off for this project. I have worked for peanuts in this national laboratory they call the best one in our country. And that's all this country can provide me until I waste a few more years trying to qualify for some bullshit exam which makes me eligible to pursue my doctorate for another five years or more. Our country looks at scientists as people who can give up all the pleasures in their life, working under egotistical seniors for ten thousand a month, when your college friends spend that much over food in a month. You then lead a life that is boring and with low expectations. So, please try to understand. I need to go out there to Europe, do my research and come back. I can join some good private company here and earn a decent salary. And trust me, we need that kind of salary in future. We both do."

The word 'future' was enough to bring a smile on Ayesha's face, and tell him that she would support him in whatever he did. It was simply that she couldn't think of him being so far away in another country.

"And no, I won't cheat on you with some European girl. I know I'm extremely good looking and tempting, but I will control my urge by giving you a phone call instead, and telling you how much I am missing you!" Piyush would answer even before she asked and get a friendly punch on his stomach.

But apparently he did yield to his urge and temptations, or that's what Ayesha had to say, when he did not receive her calls, and told her he was busy in meetings when he was out celebrating a beer fest in Berlin with his Scottish lab colleague – Kim. A girl who was pretty hot and a bitch, according to Ayesha!

He tried to cover up the lies and, later on, admitted to them, saying he did it only to keep her happy.

"Happy? Piyush, happiness depends on whether your relationship is based on truth!" "And trust!" Piyush completed her sentence.

"Trust is as important as truth, sweetheart. I agree I lied a lot of times but it all started with you doubting every move of mine. With so many insecurities that you held on to, every time I called to tell you that I was missing you, it got to a point where I lost all my patience. I have and I cannot take it anymore. You call me a cheat and it is frustrating now."

"I saw your pictures, Piyush, with that German girl of yours. Pictures don't lie, do they? I don't want to be with you anymore." Ayesha spoke with anger and tears in her eyes.

She waited for a minute of silence before slamming the phone down. That was the last phone conversation they had had as a couple.

But she was missing him like crazy now. Although she had always planned to, she could never throw his gifts away. She felt one day everything would be fine. Just the way it was. She opened her inbox and browsed through the texts he had sent and the ones she could never delete. She looked at their pictures on the laptop. She knew all this was not a step towards getting over him and the past, but tonight she simply wanted to drown in it. For one last time before she went ahead and started seeing those other guys.

She checked his Facebook profile. All she could see was his profile picture and a cover picture showing him with a couple of people. A guy and two girls had surrounded him in it. "Maybe he's dating that blonde girl on his right or maybe the Indian one on the other side," she thought looking at the picture. She couldn't help but notice the blonde girl's arm over Piyush's shoulder. Unknowingly her hand moved the cursor on the 'send a friend request' tab, and then took it away, as tears dropped on the keyboard while diving off her cheeks.

She wiped them away and suddenly heard Rocky running around.

"Rocky, no! Rocky! I said No!" Ayesha shouted twice at Rocky, trying to chase a kitten in the corridor.

Kittens! How much Piyush used to love them! As in, probably still loved them. A cat person he was! Ayesha remembered the first time when she had called Piyush home. He was about to jump over the wall seeing Rocky advance towards him.

"Please get that dog away from me. I don't like dogs, I told you."

"Hey, two things. One – I guess it's not that you don't like them. I think you are simply scared of them. And second – Rocky is not a dog. He is more like a family member. So you must like him!" Ayesha tried to control her laughter watching Piyush keeping a safe distance from Rocky.

"Okay, whatever. Just keep that sibling of yours with four legs and a tail away for a while," Piyush said and gave her a side-hug.

Then she waited for him to magically make a flower appear out of his jacket for her. Classic Piyush! He knew just too well how to put a smile on her face.

"That guy. He is not even settled yet. He is confused as to what he wants to do in his life. I am telling you, you're simply wasting your time." Ayesha's mother repeated her warning to her after her second meeting with Piyush.

But Ayesha wanted to fight for Piyush, for them both. She knew it was worth it. And eventually Piyush did get used to Rocky. And Rocky got used to Piyush. Although Ayesha and Piyush could never once agree upon which was better – Cat or a Dog.

"Rocky, what went wrong? He was a nice guy, right? You remember? You liked him too. You would go and drop him all the way to the parking lot." She spoke to her dog and he just wagged his tail in reply.

She knew he did not understand much. Maybe nothing at all. But he was her support. He had been her strength all this while. Ayesha's parents hated pets. But they could see, Rocky was the only thing that would stop her tears. And they certainly liked him more than they ever liked Piyush.

And Ayesha had nobody but Rocky to share her sorrow with. Because after a year, everyone wanted her to be okay, to be completely okay. To forget Piyush. How could that happen? To forget someone you were insanely in love with. To stop thinking of someone whose texts you woke up to, and the voice that used to be the last thing you heard before sleeping.

It was a lie. A beautiful lie. 'Move on'. Or 'Get over someone'. Terms coined by someone to publicly lie about falling out of love. Yes, she did it too. She started telling people she was getting over him now. But moving on was, in reality, colder than the break up that they had had. It was like a pact she made with everyone, to forget him when they wanted her to. In her eyes, in the mornings after long sleepless nights, in her talk and in the thousand things that reminded her of his laughter, his smile, his eyes, their kisses and their conversation.

She watched Rocky play with the cotton ball and wondered if Piyush still thought about her or not.

She had had enough for tonight. She swallowed down the tears and with a deep breath, turned off the computer. Once again she put on the TV just because she did not want Piyush to be the last thought on her mind before she tucked herself in bed. She felt he did not deserve to be that anymore.

CHAPTER 7

Being ready

Ayesha had made up her mind. She told her mother that she would look at the profiles on LetsGetMarried.com and see which guys she could meet up with and talk to.

Sad but true that our generation is caught up badly between arranged and love marriages. We grow up watching those movies and novels which throw us into a dreamland. Yes, we all want to fall in love, and we do eventually. But somehow, not all of us are able to make it last.

Most of us say out aloud how an arranged marriage is the last thing we want to go in for. But ultimately that is where most people head to with forged smiles on their faces.

Where did we go wrong? Did we fall in love too early, with the wrong people or did we get fickle along the way?

Ayesha had never thought she would end up doing this. She was never one who had approved of arranged marriages. She was the one to tell her girlfriends that not all men are assholes, and that arrange marriages should be the last thing on their mind, if they desired to have a life they dreamt of. And here she was now, seeing them transform their year or two year old relationships into a marriage.

It was like booking a *Tatkal* ticket on the Indian Railways website. At the age of 27–28, you know you are already late in booking a partner for life, which, like *Tatkal* seats, are already few in number, especially the nice ones. And then just when you decide to get the right person, you realise the kind of competition you are dealing with to get that person in time. Because if you do not, somebody else will.

Today Ayesha was meeting Guy no. 1 out of the list of guys she and her mother had shortlisted after some analysis.

Ayesha checked herself in the mirror. She had chosen to wear a *kurti* after some serious thought. She did her hair once again. She felt that she had put on some weight and then told herself it was probably her clothes that were deceptive. After applying a non shiny lip gloss and smacking her lips twice, she got away from the mirror. She suddenly felt terrible for millions of girls out there who get ready, time and time again, to see guys like this and come home dejected. She somehow felt hopeful that she wouldn't have to go through it for long.

She picked up her phone and dialled Naveen's number. Performing his duty as her best friend, he had promised her to drop her every time she went to see a guy and pick her up once she was done.

"I am waiting outside your house already. Come down fast!" he said.

Ayesha kissed her mom and dad goodbye as they wished her good luck.

"Naveen, this means a lot. I mean, are you sure you want to pick me up and drop me off every time? You never know, I might just see hundred guys. Then?" Ayesha said once she got inside Naveen's car and put on the seat belt. Pulling down the mirror on top, she checked herself once and wondered if she needed to get her eyebrows done soon.

"Yes, I know what I'm doing. And keep all the thanks to yourself. I am simply doing what I feel is right. Anyway I get bored sitting at dad's travel office.

Besides, I know how crazy you are, Ayesha. If you don't like what some guy says to you, you might hit him or something," Naveen said, giggling.

But Ayesha was too stressed to get the joke.

"I don't know, Naveen, honestly I am tense. For God's sake, I have been on dates, dates which went horribly. But I was never tense. This is crazy. Big time crazy stuff, you know. I don't even know what I'm going to say to that guy."

"You know what, Ayesha, just think you are going there as a reporter. You are doing research for your story, you know. Take it like that. That will take the burden off your heart."

"Naveen, you are not making much sense. I hope you realise that. Go there as a reporter? A story? Hahahaha!

Okay, I'm sorry. I know you're simply trying to make me feel better. I just hope everything goes well," Ayesha said, checking her phone with her painted fingernails.

"It is going be good. Who is the guy? I mean, what is his name?" Naveen asked without shifting his eyes which were firmly focused on the traffic.

"Well, let's just call him 'Guy no.1', shall we?" Ayesha said, and they both laughed.

The car moved through the old streets of the town, crossing signals and crowded streets. It took them through the roads Ayesha had grown up, learning her bicycle on. Streets where she had strolled for long hours with her friends. Her town!

"And now, here we are. Ready to meet your 'Guy no.1?' Naveen said as he slowed down the car before it came to a halt.

"Alright, good luck, Ayesha. Give me a call as soon as you are done. Okay? Cheer up!"

"Yup, thanks. I shall see you then." Ayesha waved goodbye to him and turned to Western coffee place, a small cafe that she had chosen to be the place where she would meet the guys from LetsGetMarried.com. Firstly - it served amazing coffee, and second and more importantly, very few people knew about the place. So she expected not to run across her friends over here and have to answer their barbed questions!

Telling herself that, "It's going to go just fine. It is not a big deal!" for the thirteenth time that day, she entered the cafe.

Guy No. 1

When Ayesha walked into the Western coffee place, she could feel her heartbeat was slowly getting back to normal. Probably Naveen's words of advice were not so bad, after all.

She looked around the cafe which had opened only a few years back. As she walked, she could feel that the place was bathing in an aroma of strong coffee seeds. A few waiters were carrying trays topped with coffee mugs with '*western coffee place*' embossed on them, along with some sandwiches as well. But Ayesha's eyes were searching for the guy whom she had come to visit.

She felt that today she carried a licence to ogle at men in the cafe as she looked around at them; hoping one of the better looking ones would turn out to be him. Her eyes caught a smile on the face of a strongly built man with a dusky complexion standing near the counter. She smiled back feeling relieved that good looking men did exist on matrimonial websites too. She was about to walk in his direction when, out of nowhere, came a guy, with his right hand waving at her.

"Hi! You must be Ayesha!"

Ayesha looked back at the counter only to witness that the smiling guy had disappeared.

She turned her attention back to the guy saying Hi.

"I am Guy No.1, in case you did not recognise me," he continued.

(Well, he did not exactly say his name was Guy No. 1, but that's how Ayesha heard it)

"Hi! Yes, I am Ayesha. Shall we sit and talk? Maybe… umm…that table on the left side?" she suggested to him.

"Yes, that would be fine with me. Ladies first, please," he said and watched her take a seat. And no, he did not pull out the chair for her.

"So, first of all, my full name is 'Guy no. 1'. I was born on 13th August 1985. I did my schooling from St. bla bla school and I graduated from bla bla. Then I took up a job in bla bla chemicals factory before getting promoted to bla bla…bla bla…!"

"Hello, madam and sir, can I get you anything? Some coffee and sandwiches, maybe?" said a guy who suddenly appeared like an apparition at their table, and rescued her from listening to Guy No. 1 rambling on and on. And well, he was the same guy at whom Ayesha had smiled at before. She felt a bit embarrassed.

"I will have some strong coffee and madam…well… what would you like to have?" Guy no. 1 wasn't happy that the waiter had interrupted his introduction to Ayesha.

"I'll have *cafe latte,*" spoke Ayesha, as the guy with the smile called one of the waiters and gave him the orders.

"So, as I was saying…!" Guy no. 1 simply continued his one sided dialogue with Ayesha.

While he did so, Ayesha's ears hardly let anything from that sink in, but her eyes were busy profiling this Guy no. 1. Her mind was analysing his dressing sense and the way he talked.

He was wearing a checked blue tie over a multicoloured striped shirt and trousers worn over his belly. He looked like a medical representative, who had come to the clinic to sell a new lot of medicines.

He was carrying a black shoulder bag along, which gave his salesman look a finishing touch. Ayesha felt as if she herself had come to buy an insurance policy or something.

His next action woke her up from her thoughts.

He took the black bag on his lap and from it he removed, what looked like a form.

"Now before you say I talk too much, I would like to ask you a few questions," he said looking at Ayesha. When he said that, he did not smile. Not even a smirk. He was way too serious about the whole getting to know each other thing.

"I think asking each other about hobbies and all has become too mainstream. So I have prepared a questionnaire. It has a set of questions, each carrying a different weight or marks."

"And what do you plan to do with it?" Ayesha was really taken aback. "Is this an interview or something?"

"I like the way you treat it, Madam. I do. Yes, consider it as one," He said, smiling at the expression of surprise on Ayesha's face.

"Here is your *cafe latte,* madam and here is your *strong coffee,* sir," again interrupted the waiter, this time a different one. Ayesha searched around for the former guy who took the order, and found him standing at the other end, but still with a smile on his face. She turned her attention to the mug of *cafe latte* with hot chocolate dancing on espresso and topped with skimmed milk. She touched the mug to her lips as the first sip of coffee slid down her tongue.

"So, as I was saying, I will now ask you some questions."

"Yes, please do" Ayesha felt like laughing but wanted to go all the way before she could make fun of it.

"Miss Ayesha, do you feel you have made all right decisions in the past?"

"Well, not really. It must have been a mixture of right and wrong, with wrong ones teaching me more actually," Ayesha answered.

"Okay fine. Second question! Which one is more important, according to you? Work life or social life? Think carefully before you answer!"

Ayesha could not stifle a smirk on her face with this question, but managed to answer it somehow, "I think we need to strive to achieve a balance between both. It's a difficult task but both are equally important." "That is the right answer. Now, next question!" Guy no. 1 now sported a kind of smile on his face that said he had met an intelligent candidate for his interview after a long time.

Ayesha decided she would give her full attention and try to remember as many questions as she could, so that she could go back and laugh at them with Naveen.

Guy no. 1 wasn't done yet. He kept asking her a series of questions. It reminded her of the job interviews she had faced earlier. She felt those were somehow better than this one. Looking at him asking questions so sincerely, at one point of time, she wanted to appreciate him for his hard work on making such a detailed questionnaire. The next moment she felt like this must be part of some big prank being played on her, and that everyone in the cafe would be involved in it.

"Now we come to an important part!" Guy no. 1 said, raising his eyebrows and one hand.

"The end?" Ayesha couldn't hold back her sarcasm anymore.

"No, the last question. And it carries maximum marks," he said without letting the grave expression go off his face.

"Okay. And does it mean that you marry the girl with the maximum score in your…umm…this test?"

"Kind of. And I must tell you are doing really well," he said and continued.

"Tell me what you will do if you are trapped on an aeroplane which has caught fire?"

"Hmm. That is a difficult question. I think I will put on an oxygen mask if there are fumes and it's difficult to move around. I'll keep my patience and listen to the announcements done by the airlines staff. I'll try and figure out which are the nearest exit routes in case of a bad landing."

"That is a good answer again," Guy no. 1 did not hide his satisfaction over her answer this time.

The black envelope carrying the bill arrived at the table and Guy no. 1 insisted on paying the full amount. But she won the small debate and they split the bill.

"So, I will…"

"Yes, let me know if I passed the exam," Ayesha completed his sentence and waved him goodbye.

Ayesha had already started laughing even before she got into Naveen's car.

"You have no idea what happened inside," she said, one hand holding her stomach while laughing.

She then narrated the entire story to Naveen on their way back home.

"You do realise, you passed his exam right?" Naveen gave her a look of askance.

"Yeah, I guess. How does it matter? I am not marrying him."

"I know you are not. But he will call you soon, thinking you will. What will you say then, why not?"

"I'll just say something. Oh my God, Naveen, I did not think of that. What do I say?"

"Chill! Just say that your *kundli* does not match with his or something."

"Wow. Mr Naveen, you know a lot about these things. Did you also secretly open a matrimony account, hmm?" she nudged him in a friendly manner.

"Hahaha ,no. Just heard so from people. *Kundli* is the most common excuse that people use on such occasions."

"Hmm, yeah, it may come in handy. You are right, buddy," Ayesha replied, while taking the seat belt off and getting out of the car.

"Bye!" they both said together, and headed towards their respective homes.

Naveen was right. Guy no. 1 did call her the very next day. She did not even answer his first two calls, simply because she did not know how to say no. When she finally touched the green answering tab on her phone, he hurriedly told that she had passed the questionnaire test, and that he was ready to marry her.

"But don't you believe in *Kundli* and all?" she asked him.

"Oh no, all that is archaic now. What really matters is 'the compatibility'. And you scored really high on the test," he answered.

"I'm very religious and I strongly believe in *kundli* matching," she gave out the well rehearsed answer.

"Oh!" he was taken by surprise.

"And I'm sorry to let you know that you did not pass that exam," she said, before hanging up the phone.

She did feel bad for rejecting him like that, but what other choice did she have? She herself felt like quitting the whole matrimony thing right away. But somehow she convinced herself not to. It was too early to. So she made up her mind and decided to meet the second guy.

She picked up the Earnest Hemmingway novel that she had left half finished, and complemented it with a mug of custom made coffee. She did not like the idea of half-finished things. Before she could pull out the bookmark, her cell phone screen smiled with a bright light and displayed '*Nisha calling*' on its face. Ayesha answered the call and spoke to her for a long time, about her job, Nisha's married life, sex life, shopping, and everything except 'her being part of the matrimony world'. Nisha told her that Piyush had come back to India and had taken up a job at one of the big pharmaceuticals. Ayesha did not need to hear that. Nisha did not need to say that. It was not the right time.

Ayesha did not like the idea of half-finished things. Once again the Earnest Hemmingway novel was going to be left unread for a while.

Chapter 8

"Sir, I would need a Saturday off this week," Ayesha told her boss in a polite manner on Friday evening.

"Oh, I'm afraid that won't be possible," he said, watching her pack her bags for the day. He continued, "I don't know how it skipped my mind today, to let you know that tomorrow morning, we have planned a small seminar for our lifestyle magazine. How can it take place without you being there?"

"Ohh, I see. Not an issue, Sir. I shall be there!" Ayesha gave the perfect reply.

"Well, you can leave early though. It should not take that long," He said, as she smiled and left the office.

"Now I have to reschedule my meeting with the matrimony guy to evening," she spoke to herself, as her car took a steep turn out of the basement parking lot.

"Saturday evenings are meant for dates, not matrimony matters. Damn it!" she thought, as she remembered that she had not even had a 'girls night out' for a long time. Either her job had distanced her from a lot of people, or maybe she chose it to do so, in order to stay away from the world of her recently married schoolmates and college friends.

But now she needed their company. She needed to gossip like a regular girl. Go to malls, try out tops and later on, buy similar ones from the roadside shops for a much lower price. She needed to do Malibu coconut rum shots with them again and push the vodka down her throat. She needed to rejuvenate herself. But that would have to wait, she knew it. First, she had to meet the next contestant for the game of marriage. She had just prepared herself for that.

Guy No. 2

"So that was all about '*Grandeur*', our Lifestyle magazine, and now, allow me to hand over the microphone to our Senior Editor, Miss Ayesha!" Mr Gulati ended his speech, which was met with a round of applause from the audience.

Ayesha adjusted her ocean blue *sari* and stepped up on the podium. Holding the microphone in her left hand, she glanced across the seminar hall lit with bright lights and an audience of thirty to forty seated in front of her eyes.

"Good afternoon, everyone! I would like to thank Gulati sir and all my seniors, as well as colleagues, for providing me with this wonderful opportunity. We all have worked hard for the success of this newspaper, and I'm honoured to be able to contribute to the same. I can assure you all that *Grandeur* will be nothing but success. Our market research group, our media agency and the writing staff has already been working hard for our magazine to have a grand launch…" Ayesha then concluded the seminar with a series of 'thank you' messages to several contributors to the lifestyle magazine. It was certainly a moment of pride for her.

After having satiated her rumbling tummy with snacks and a cold drink, she asked her boss for permission to leave for the day. He happily granted one. Ayesha was an asset to their company and they simply could not risk losing her, let alone keep her unhappy at the job.

Ayesha swiped her right thumb across the smart phone to check if there were any calls or texts that she had missed during the seminar. Naveen had texted her a big 'sorry' saying he would not be able to accompany her to the cafe, but that he would surely come and meet her once he was done with his office work later in the night. Replying a full 'okay' to it, she tucked herself inside her Hyundai i20 and put on the seat belt. Igniting the engine, she wondered if it was a good idea to meet the matrimony guy in this condition – wearing a *sari.* She wasn't particularly a fan of wearing one, even though a lot of people had complimented her today, saying how pretty she looked in it. "A *Sari* is more revealing than most clothes. I do not know why they keep bad-mouthing western clothes," she would say to her mother. But then her mother had taught her perfectly, how to drape it without anything being seen or revealed. So she thanked her mother in her head, while her cell phone screen flashed on the seat next to her. It was the Matrimony guy. It seemed like he had already reached the *Western coffee place.* She gently pressed her right foot on the accelerator and the speed-O-meter reacted in response. "A few minutes more and I'll be talking to my probable future husband!" She laughed at her own thought.

At the *Western coffee place*

"Hi! You are Miss Ayesha, right?" a thinly built guy, looking like someone who just graduated, came up to her and said as soon as she walked in.

"Hi, Yes, I am. And you are Guy no.2 right?"

"Yes, you guessed it right," he said, accompanied by a weird laughter that Ayesha chose to ignore.

"Shall we sit?" Ayesha asked, feeling uncomfortable standing there in that *sari.*

"Yes, yes, okay!" he said, not being able to hide his nervousness on speaking to a good looking girl.

As they walked across the cafe towards her usual table, she could sense him checking her from head to toe. She wanted to hate him for that, but then she herself had done it half a minute back.

He wore a dark blue shirt which still had vertical folds across, letting her know that he must have worn it for the first time since he bought it. The guy had neatly combed his hair and probably used too much of shampoo, which was noticeable from his receding hairline.

Making herself comfortable, she watched him as he wiped sweat off his forehead. It reminded her of her college days. This surely was not the first time she had intimidated a guy with her personality. So she just gave him some more time to get settled at the place and allowed him to speak first.

"First of all, I would like to say that I'm really happy seeing you like this." He managed his first sentence at last.

"Like this?" Ayesha spoke as he said that.

"I meant in a *sari*. You know, very few girls respect our traditional attire these days. I am really glad that you are one of them."

"Well, before you make any of those assumptions, let me tell you…!" Ayesha did not expect this.

"No, you don't really have to explain yourself. I do get it. I understand that most probably you are wearing a *sari* because you have come here to see me. But I still appreciate it. I do."

"Well…umm…whatever," Ayesha blurted out, as she really did not care enough about what he thought the reason was.

"Would you like me to take the order for you?" interrupted the waiter while handing over the menu to them.

"Yes, *cafe latte* for me and …what will you have, Guy no.2?" she had been craving for caffeine ever since she left the seminar hall.

"I will have the same as Madam is having," he said, smiling nervously at the waiter.

"Hmm…So, you are working as an editor at Daily Chronicle?"

"Yes. Senior Editor actually. I recently got promoted."

"Oh, congratulations. That's wonderful news."

"Thank you. What do you do?" Ayesha asked, feeling slightly bad that she had not even read his bio before coming to meet him.

"I…I am a project manager at T & L steel firm. I did my engineering from C.O.E.P. College. And other than that, I like to play cricket. I have even represented my college at inter college cricket tournaments. "

"Good to know!" Ayesha replied, while she tore off another packet of sugar and poured it into her coffee. The heart shaped cream on top dispersed into milk as she did that.

"And you want to talk about anything else besides hobbies?" he asked her, wondering if he was talking too much about himself…so much unlike the Guy no. 1.

"Well, what are your expectations from your future wife? What are the things, the qualities that you are looking for?" she said the first thing that came to her mind. She really did not plan to put any more stress on her already tired mind after the morning's seminar.

"I…I would want her, I mean I hope she will be understanding, religious, one who respects family values and can perform basic domestic duties."

"Okay, and by domestic duties, you mean?" Ayesha almost did not care if the tone of her voice sounded rude.

"You know, basic cooking, attending guests, helping elders at home… all that. What are your views about religion?" he asked with a lot more confidence than his body language had displayed when he shook hands with her ten minutes back.

"I am a non believer. You can say that and there is no shame. I do not hate God but I do not understand him or her either. So, no, I do not worship, don't go to temples or mosques or churches. And yes, I do not follow Satan either. Don't worry!" Ayesha cleared her mind, realising she had gone a bit too far with the last line.

"Ohh, okay. Hmm…!" Guy no. 2 was back to wiping sweat off his forehead with that answer.

"Well, honestly speaking, my family is very religious. And we expect our daughter in law as well to be so. I mean my parents do. So, would you be able to do that?" Guy no. 2

spoke as he could see she was fast escaping from his future wife criterion.

"I am sorry. But since I don't believe in it, I do not see a reason to do that. I respect your faith and do not ask you to stop worshipping whatever you believe in. So, I do expect the same freedom,"

"Okay. I see. And what about dressing? I mean, is it okay if you have to let go of wearing western clothes? Because my father does not approve of them."

"Can I ask you something, Guy no. 2?" Ayesha spoke looking straight at his eyes.

"Yes, please do."

"Whatever you wrote in your bio on the matrimonial website or whatever you spoke about the qualities that you are looking for in the girl you wish to marry, were those decided by you or your parents? No offence. I'm just asking."

"Well, I would say, both. But my parents have looked after me till the time I started earning. They raised me. I have to respect their views. I will marry the girl who fits into that criterion."

"Okay, I respect the fact that you are so obedient and respectful towards your parents. But all I am saying is that a girl has some wishes too. She herself is leaving her family and coming to stay with you, like you said you want her to. So, you know, girls look for a guy who can stand up for them at times at least." Ayesha talked to him as if she was advising one of her office colleagues over their relationship issues.

"I get it, Miss Ayesha. But that is how I want to go ahead with this. I do not see anything wrong with it and I am sorry but I do not think we are compatible. I don't think it is a good thing for us to go ahead with it. Unless you know, you change your mind and are ready to perform some domestic and religious duties."

"Are you going to change your mind and stop worshipping your God?" Ayesha's retort was waiting to bounce back.

"No," answered Guy no. 2 as they paid the bill.

Without saying anything further to each other, they both left the coffee place.

Ayesha's mind was filled with mixed feelings. She did not know whether she had come here to see a guy for marriage, or to win a debate over orthodox culture and freedom of dressing views. She loathed men who prohibited their wives and girlfriends from dressing in a way they wished to. She had seen numerous examples of the same in her recently married friends and colleagues. She remembered some of her friends telling her how their long time boyfriends turned husbands suddenly started whining over them wearing shorts and knee length dresses in some cases. "Yes, it is necessary to dress as per the occasion and area where you are, but completely wanting your wife to wear saris and suits totally sucked," she felt.

"Peep…Peep…," a vehicle from behind honked and a cloud of thoughts over Ayesha's head burst through. She turned her car towards the North flyover and decided to pick up a Subway sandwich for herself and her father on the way back home.

CHAPTER 9

The Lazy Sunday

Sundays are under-rated. Highly, I believe. I mean people start celebrating the arrival of Saturday right from Friday evening itself. But Sundays are all about crying over 'the next week starting tomorrow' thing. People are, alas, more vocal about Monday blues than they are when it comes to asking someone out on Saturday night.

In Ayesha's case yesterday, the Saturday was all about Guy no. 2 and his religious views. She had slept only after a long discussion she had had with her father over the same. Her father intermittently attempted in vain to change the topic of conversation to the seminar she had had. But then he had to raise the white flag, while they both relished the *Aachari Chicken* Subways Ayesha had parcelled for them.

"Hey, good morning, lazy bird" Ayesha managed to pick up Naveen's call after trying to swap her finger across the touch screen thrice.

"Morning, Naveen!" she spoke with half opened sleepy eyes.

"So what's up? Are we meeting up? You never even told me how it went with your Guy no. 2? You were supposed to call me," Naveen asked her curiously.

"Hehehe. Naveen, stop sounding like a girl who is dying to hear some gossip. And yes, let's catch up over lunch."

"Hmm, Okay. Where do you want to go? George Restaurant? We can have some good *Biryani* or something," Naveen replied.

"Alright, Mister Naveen. Let us do as you say. But that means I need to get out of this bed and inform my mother before she cooks anything for me. Urrrgh!"

"Haha! You do that. Get fresh. I shall come and pick you up around 1 o'clock. See you!"

"See you. Tata!"

Ayesha got up and got ready faster than a kitten that would jump up when it smelt its favourite food.

"Hop in!" Naveen said to Ayesha, stretching his left hand to open the car door.

"Oh, nice shades, dude!" she said looking at his newly bought glares as she got into the car.

The car moved unusually slowly that day, in spite of the less crowded roads, since Ayesha and Naveen had so much to talk about.

"So how are aunty and uncle doing? Everything good at home?" Naveen asked as they reached the place.

"They are good. And they never pressurise me. I love them for that. You know, ever since the time I started doing this whole 'seeing guys for marriage' thing, I cannot stop feeling bad for millions of girls out there who are burdened with pressure to get married from their families."

"I agree. It is a pretty sad situation for them. We can't help that, can we?" Naveen said, while scrolling his eyes across the menu card.

"*Pasta primavera* with red sauce for me. And yes a cosmopolitan too," Ayesha did not need a menu card for her order.

"Hmm, so, how did the big seminar go, Miss Editor?" Naveen intentionally asked her about seminar first, knowing that she needed to talk about something good first.

"It was wonderful. It couldn't have been better. There were praises, heaps of praises. There were responsibilities, but overall it was fantastic. In fact, my next whole week is all action packed."

"What kind of action, ha ha?" Naveen laughed out.

"*Arey*, I mean we are having a promotional tour for our newly launched magazine next week. For that, we'll be travelling to all the metro cities. First Delhi, then Kolkata, Bangalore and then back to Mumbai. I will be staying there with my colleagues, one day at every city. It is going to be hectic, but I'm excited. Phewww!" Ayesha spoke at a length.

"Yummy, hmm…try this, Naveen," she said, taking a bite of garlic bread that came as a complimentary dish.

"So, tell me about the Guy no. 2. I mean tell me how you turned him down, eh?" Naveen tried some sarcasm with humour.

"Turned him down? It was mutual. Beat that!" Ayesha spoke.

"Hahaha, what are you saying? What did you do?"

"Well, I was just being myself. That's what I did. The guy did not belong to our time. That is what happened," she said.

Naveen shook his head as he took a sip of iced tea and let her continue.

"The guy was completely orthodox. I happened to go there in a *sari* because of my seminar, and he took that as a sign of my respect towards traditional attire and what not. That is fine. But then, he expects his future wife to perform so called 'domestic duties' with which, basically, he wouldn't be ready to sully his hands. Then of course, he was taken aback when I disclosed my atheistic side to him. And we both ended up walking off. Chapter closed."

"Wow! I never thought you'll come across such a guy. Well, you can't really blame the guy. I mean it's not his fault that your views don't match with his, right? Maybe he has simply been brought up like that."

"Thank you, Naveen, for taking his side. You want me to set you up with him?" Ayesha made an angry expression at him with a fork in her hand.

"No, I'm happy being single as of now. Anyway tell me, so next week you'll be out travelling. Then what about the next guy? When are you planning to meet him?"

"Oh, let me live. I shall meet him next Monday. This week I want to take my mind completely off this marriage thing."

"You are right. And you never know, you might just meet your future husband during this trip. What say?" Naveen suggested.

"You are so sweet, Naveen. I hope so. But we are still splitting the bill," Ayesha said with a smirk on her face.

"Yes, Ayesha, bad joke seriously," Naveen said as they passed the cheque to the waiter.

The next week was, indeed, hectic, yet exciting. She went to all the cities, attended conferences and participated in seminars. She attended exhibitions and caught up with old friends in their respective towns. It went very well. But no, she did not meet her future husband on the one week long trip. Maybe because she was not meant to! Not yet!

Guy No. 3

At *Western coffee place*

This time Ayesha was the one waiting for the guy from LetsGetMarried.com to come to the cafe. She had taken her usual table around the corner. Sitting there, she couldn't help but tap her fingers nervously on the table top while waiting for the guy to arrive.

And then he did. Guy no. 3!

She stared at him from head to toe. When you are trying to get married and meeting unknown people for it, it is completely fair to do so.

He looked like he was wearing formal clothes for the first time, as he pulled his trousers twice and adjusted the belt on his waist. His clothes were a bit shabby too. She saw that his hair was slightly messed up. And then he saw her and came walking towards her, at an unusually fast pace.

"Hey, Hi…I am…"

"Guy no. 3? I know, please sit down. And yes, I am Ayesha," she said hurriedly.

"Wow, this is true," he said taking a look around the coffee place and people.

"I am sorry, what is true?" Ayesha questioned him, noticing for the first time how glassy his eyes were.

"It is true. I mean, have you ever been on a blind date, Ayesha?"

"Umm…I do not see how that is related to this?" Ayesha was baffled with the question.

"Well, never mind!" he said and took a seat. He then continued,

"Blind date and this, 'seeing people for marriage' thing is almost the same. Isn't it? I mean, on a blind date, you walk into a bar or a cafe or wherever your friends have set you up with someone. Then you take a look around, hoping that it is one of the good looking people sitting there. But hey, are we not forgetting the fact that if it had to be a good looking person, why would they need a blind date in the first place?"

"Okay. Go on," Ayesha said, not realising that she was nodding along.

Guy no. 3 went on speaking,

"So, isn't this almost the similar case where we see each other, and make up our minds in almost the first few minutes? The remaining part of the meeting is a mere formality."

"Yes, maybe. Yes, I guess I'm going to have to agree with you on that part." Ayesha realised that the glassy eyed guy was, in fact, much more interesting than the ones she had met before from the matrimony website.

"And I am getting a sense of déjà vu looking at you. I am not going to throw the mashed up pick up line that I think I have seen you before. But hey, what you know? Maybe we did meet in the parallel universe. Maybe we are even dating each other already out there. You believe in a parallel universe, right? And what about the string theory?" Guy no. 3 had just started sounding creepier and less interesting now.

"I am not sure of that," Ayesha realised that there was something wrong with this guy. And his eyes, she remembered she had seen those kinds of eyes before.

"Is he stoned?" she asked herself.

"What are your thoughts on the legalisation of marijuana?" she said before she thought.

"Umm…Yes. Exactly, yes. I think it is time. You think so too?" He said, and without waiting for her answer, continued to speak.

"In fact, you're so pretty that I'm having a difficult time sinking into reality after these marijuana hallucinations," he said and then, took a pause for a minute. He understood her sarcasm. He then spoke, "Hey, listen, I am sorry I did not mean to smoke up today, but my friend asked me to and then I was too stoned to refuse the offer. I hope you understand."

"Hmm! How often do you smoke up anyway, if I may ask?" Ayesha's tone sounded more like his mother's now.

"Well, depends on the…I mean, twice or thrice a day," he admitted.

"And you think that is good or what?" Ayesha felt like she was interviewing a spoiled teenaged cousin of hers.

"It is bad. Be it once or twice, I know. But I guess my engineering days got me addicted to it. I had, in fact, quit it last year. I did not do it for almost two to three months. But whenever you get free time, and friends who are under its influence, you tend to succumb to the temptation."

"That is okay, as long as you are aware of it," she said, letting him talk.

"In fact, it is my first time to come and see a girl for marriage. I am not even sure if I am ready for this. Maybe we can meet up again, get to know each other. You know, we can be in a relationship for some time and then decide. Is that okay with you?" He spoke as his eyes made some sense for the first time that evening.

"I do not think that is a good idea. I do not even have that amount of time with me anyway. But you know what?" Ayesha said to him, "I think you can get over the habit quite soon. That will give you a good amount of time to get back to the real world. And then you can give a serious thought to whether you are ready for a marriage or not".

"I think so too. You are a really good person, Ayesha. I strongly feel so. Thank you! Someone else in your position would have freaked out by now. I think I shall do that. I had decided anyway to quit it as soon as college gets over. Now that I'm working, I really need to. Thanks!" he smiled as he spoke.

Ayesha had finished her *cafe latte* long time back. She smiled back at him and asked the waiter for the bill.

After she said bye to the Guy no. 3, she dialled Naveen's number on the phone.

"Hey, Ayesha, I'm already waiting outside." Naveen said before she could say hello.

After locating Naveen's car from the mesh of traffic on the road, she threw her bag on the back seat and relaxed on the seat next to him.

"So, how was it? Any better than the previous guy?" Naveen asked her on their way back.

"It was fine. Naveen, can I ask you something?"

"Yes, go on," Naveen said with a look of askance.

"Do you believe in a parallel universe?"

"Why are you asking me that?" Naveen said, bemused.

"Never mind! Just like that," Ayesha chuckled, looking outside the window at the moon that was chasing their car.

Chapter 10

The moon that had been chasing their car was now standing firm in the window frame of Ayesha's bedroom. Her thoughts were still on 'the parallel universe' and the thought lingered in her mind about whether it really did exist or not.

No, it wasn't because she was persuaded to believe so by Guy no. 3. It wasn't the first time she had heard about it. Science and Fiction had been Piyush's favourite subjects and her favourite stories. She loved to be enthralled, listening to him talk passionately about theories of origin of the universe and time travel. Especially, the latter! She liked to make fun of Piyush, every time he told her how strongly he believed that the Time machine would exist in future and that maybe, they were simply unaware of them travelling back in time. How she wished now that it was true. She badly needed a time machine. She did.

"By the way I do not believe in a parallel universe, hehe!" The message from Naveen on her phone read. She felt bad at times for him being so good to her. She felt people needed to have some faults as well. Especially, guys who were too nice! A man needed to be a bit of an asshole as well. "That is what attracts us to them in the first place. So, later on we can say, 'you know he is a bit naughty and sarcastic, but he really cares for me'". Naveen was a good momma's boy on the other hand.

And he had been extremely supportive and helpful to her throughout the 'seeing guys for marriage thing'. Was mother right in telling me to spare a thought for him? He was a true gentleman. And yes, they both knew each other from childhood, had spent so much time together. He knew everything she did, does and wanted to be. There was no need or room to hide anything. And on top of that, the guy genuinely liked her. "But again, he is my friend. Oh, what am I even thinking?" she whisked herself away from those thoughts and logged into her multiple social networking accounts.

It is funny how we have different status updates for each one of them. It is like we are living different lives and different personalities at a time. Today her timeline showed another wedding album uploaded by one of her schoolmates. And it wasn't the guy that girl had been going around with for almost a decade. "But somehow she looks happy, doesn't she?" Ayesha tried to search for some optimism through it. Then she moved the wheel of the mouse down to come to a photo a few of her friends had commented on. Piyush was sitting at a pizza place, a familiar place actually. "Oh, it is the one next to Naveen's house!" she exclaimed, as she realised he was in town. He looked a bit healthier and even more handsome than before. And a bigger asshole than he had been with his arms around a new girl this time. Screw it! She told herself and diverted her mind. She was happy that she was doing a lot better now with the 'getting over' part.

The still-unfinished novel from the edge of her computer table caught her attention and she decided to do justice to it. Shutting down all the browser windows, she picked up the book and put on her glasses. “A novel a day, keeps lame memories away!” written on her bookmark was enough to put a smile on her face.

Chapter 11

Wednesday Morning at the Daily Chronicle

That day, as soon as Ayesha reached her office, she was greeted first, not just by the receptionist, but also with the bouquet of flowers in her hands.

"Oh, thank you, sweetie!" Ayesha was surprised.

"It is not from me. A guy had come here sometime back. He gave these flowers for you and yes, left a note for you. Here!" the receptionist said, pointing to a note on the side.

"What did he say his name was?" Ayesha was surprised in a happy way.

"He did not say anything. But I guess, it must be there on the note,"

"Yeah, you are right. Thank you anyway. And do not tell anyone else about this," Ayesha warned her in a friendly tone.

Ayesha took the bouquet in her hand and walked to her cabin, hoping that no one would ask her about the same. She succeeded.

At her cabin she couldn't stop herself from checking the note as soon as she had placed the flowers delicately on the table.

"*To Ayesha,*

Hoping this is the first of many times I make you smile.

From..."

"From Guy no. 4" Ayesha read it and smiled. She had not imagined something like this would happen in her wildest dream.

And that wasn't the only time he made her smile. Soon she got a text from him asking her if she had received the flowers. She replied saying she liked them, omitting the part that it really did make her smile. She wanted to keep it formal at least till the time she met the guy.

She did not have to wait that long. A meeting was scheduled for the next evening, the place being...well of course the same - *Western coffee place.*

Guy No. 4

Chapter 12

The first 'matrimony' guy that made her smile!

Naveen dropped Ayesha at the coffee place and saw her saying goodbye happily for the first time. She seemed hopeful about this guy somehow. For the first time, Naveen questioned his own decision to drop her and pick her up this way every time. He was human after all, and someone who loved Ayesha more than anybody else he had known. Maybe the time had come to say goodbye to her soon, and to watch her walk down the aisle with some man, with her man. Not him. How would his parents react, and his friends? They would just laugh at him. He felt Piyush was a better man for her to end up with. He remembered how many people had tried to persuade him to ask Ayesha out after she broke up with Piyush. Maybe they were right, maybe not. In the dilemma, he reversed the car and pushed the accelerator up as he left the road.

Here at *Western coffee place*, Ayesha was waiting for the guy no. 4 to show up fast. He did not disappoint her.

"Hey there, Ayesha, right? How are you doing?"

"Hi, Guy no. 4. I am doing great. And you?" Ayesha so much wanted this cute looking guy to say yes.

"Good. Me too," he said and Ayesha found it difficult to stifle the smile on her lips.

"Shall we take the table around the corner?" he said pointing to her favourite table.

"Yeah, that would be good," she said with pseudo formality.

"I hope the flowers did not freak you out. I mean, I know gifts can be creepy at times," he initiated the conversation like an intelligent man.

"Oh no, not at all. They were good. Thank you!" Ayesha said. She wanted to tell him that she loves gifts, but knew it was too early to say that.

He called the waiter and asked her what she would like to have.

"*Cafe latte* for Madam, I believe, and Sir, what would you like to have?" the cafe waiter said with more confidence than Ayesha would have liked.

She kept her eyes fixed on Guy no. 4 as he placed his order and waited for the waiter to leave.

"So, I believe we have both read each other's basic information and hobbies and what we are looking for. So to cut a long piece short, what would you like to know about me?" Guy no. 4 asked her.

"Umm…well…what I wish to know…," Ayesha pretended to think it over although she already had a question lingering in her mind.

"Okay, tell me, why an arranged marriage?"

"Hmm…!" he took a deep breath, followed by a sip of coffee, and answered.

"An arranged marriage because…because honestly speaking, the love marriage did not work out."

With that answer, suddenly his cute face turned sad and he tried not to look into her eyes.

"Oh, I am sorry if the question bothers you. You do not have to answer it," she said.

"No, no. It is fine. I anyway planned to discuss it with you. It makes sense to share that part with someone who could be your future wife," he replied.

"Oh, I just realised that sounds a bit weird – saying 'future wife,'" he corrected himself before she could react.

"Haha, no, that is fine. Yes you were telling me something, go on!" Ayesha tried to create a comfort zone for him to speak out.

"Yes," he said taking another sip of already turning cold-coffee in his mug to buy some time for himself.

"Well, I was in a relationship with this girl. For almost three years. Three and half actually," he said, finally lifting his head to look into Ayesha's eyes.

"We both were madly in love with each other. Kiran – that was her name! I met her through a common friend at a friend's party, and after that, we never looked back. She was a mass media student. I was doing my architecture course. We shared our dreams and supported each other. She believed in me, she always did. Until one day when I told her my plans to open up a Sports bar and a lounge after completing the architecture degree. She felt I had gone crazy and asked me to reconsider it. I did not. She felt I should work in the field of architecture since I had put so many years of my life into studying it. But for me, I could not give up on my dream of a sports lounge, since everything was falling into place for me. After her mass media course, she joined the production house, while I on the other hand, refused every architecture job that came my way. She tried her best to dissuade me from the same. She failed. And for her, I failed. After a series of fights and arguments, we broke up," he said.

"And that is my story of a failed attempt at love-marriage. You know the rest! I am sitting here trying to make an arranged marriage work," he said trying to cover the grief with a plastic smile.

"I am really sorry to hear that," Ayesha could not think of a better reply.

"But on the positive note, the lounge that I opened is running quite successfully. It is getting a very good response from college students and sport-enthusiasts. We have recently got additional screens to screen football matches live for our customers along with good music. They love it. Anyway, tell me, what are your views on the same? Did I do something wrong?" He asked her finally.

"Well, with all due respect to what your girlfriend thought, I agree with what you did. I think you followed your heart. You felt there was good sense in opening up a lounge, and you were right. What is wrong with that? You should not feel sad. Things happen. You are a successful entrepreneur at this age. Very few people can stand up and say that," Ayesha said more than she thought she would.

"Thanks. Thanks for the support. So, you believe only in arranged marriages?" he asked her the question despite knowing the answer.

"Not really. In fact, I never thought I would be going to a matrimony website and doing all this," Ayesha felt much more comfortable talking to the guy no. 4 now.

"I also went through a relationship. I was in a serious relationship with a guy for a long time. Everything was going on right, as long as he was here. Then he went to Europe for further studies and we started having differences. Like in your case, a series of fights followed and one day we broke up. The end!"

"Hmm! That happens. But isn't it a good thing for two such people to meet up? I mean, we both have gone through it, we both have that required part of 'understanding'. I mean, not everyone can deal with a person who comes with baggage, right?" Guy no. 4 said what she wanted to hear.

"Yes, you are right. And especially through these matrimony websites! Hahaha!" she said and both of them laughed.

"You know the last guy I met was a total...," Ayesha narrated the funny experience she had had on meeting guy no. 3 and the ones before that.

He told her some of the weird stuff he went through as well, while meeting one girl through a matrimony website. He told her how that girl kept chasing him wherever he went for almost three months, even after he had told her that his answer was no.

They got so engrossed in the conversation that it became time for the cafe guy to come up to them and let them know that it was time to close for the day.

Outside, on the opposite side of the road, Naveen had been waiting in his car for Ayesha to come out, secretly hoping that she had rejected guy no. 4.

To Naveen's disappointment, Ayesha had not rejected guy no. 4. If fact, she was thinking of meeting him again. She did not tell Naveen that. But she did tell him that she liked this guy, and there was a faint chance that she could give it a thought. Naveen replied with a cold 'okay' to that. She hardly noticed his displeasure as she was busy watching the moon outside chasing their car once again. Today it looked romantic to her.

As soon as she reached home, she hugged her mother and told her that she might have just met the right guy. Her mother was a bit sceptical as she was afraid of her daughter going through another heart-break. But she managed to smile and listened to her entire story. She asked Ayesha to be patient and take things slowly. Ayesha kissed her on her forehead and said, "As you say momma!" and rushed to her room.

Changing into comfortable shorts, she lay down on the bed with eyes closed, yet seeing so many things. She asked herself a couple of times, whether the guy was really that cute looking, and every time a pleasant 'yes' was the answer. The things she liked the most about him were his honesty and the fact that he knew how to treat a woman. The way he greeted her, the way he spoke with confidence and those flowers. Wow, how long it had been since someone had gifted her something? A fairly long time really. She liked how he had texted her asking if she had reached home safely. She felt like someone cared enough to treat her as special after a long time, after Piyush had gone from her life.

Ayesha felt a bit sad thinking she was letting some guy into her life, a guy other than Piyush. But the very next moment, she remembered his pictures with other girls, with his arms around their necks. It is time to move on, she reminded herself.

She decided to meet guy no. 4 again in the next few days. She felt there was lot more that they had to talk about and share, before things could go ahead. Ayesha remembered how quickly his smile turned to sorrow when he started talking about his past relationship. She needed a guy like him who would understand and respect her past. She wondered why his girl friend had broken up with such a cute guy over a silly reason. With random thoughts dancing in her head, she pushed the button on the TV remote control. '*Notting hill*' her favourite movie was coming on HBO. She tucked her feet properly inside the quilt and raised the volume.

Chapter 13

Catching up

Ayesha checked herself twice in the mirror from right, straight and from left angle. She put on lip gloss and pressed her lips gingerly for it to spread well. Nisha had called for the second time in the past two minutes.

"Ayesha, come down quickly. I am waiting"

"Yes, just locking the door," Ayesha said, searching for the keys to the lock.

Finally, after another two minutes, she was downstairs. Nisha stepped in front and both hugged each other after almost six months or more. Six months since the day Nisha had married Amit, her long time boyfriend. They were one of the couples at college, whom no one had thought would stay on together after a few years. To everyone's surprise, they did. And Nisha went all the way to marry him, and then moved to Delhi where his family stayed. A perfect love turned into an arranged marriage. So freaking ideal, or was it? Ayesha was about to discover, as they marched toward their favourite sizzlers' place nearby.

"So, how is everyone at home?" Ayesha asked her as they walked on the left side of the road.

"Oh, everyone is doing fine. You tell me, how is everything?" Nisha asked her.

"Great. Did I tell you I got promoted?" Ayesha held Nisha's shoulder and spoke like a happy school going kid.

"No. But great news, girl! Congratulations. You deserved it anyway," Nisha said and they walked inside the restaurant.

An aroma of hot and spicy sauces from somewhere inside the kitchen welcomed them both and tickled their hungry stomachs.

"Let us sit upstairs," Ayesha dominated the decision making process as usual, and started walking upstairs without waiting for Nisha to respond.

Nisha walked behind her and so did the waiter.

"You know I'm coming here after such a long time. I miss this place. Actually a lot of things," Nisha spoke while taking a seat.

"I know, same here. I love this place. And I hardly get to come here despite it being so close to my house."

"You are in touch with Piyush? You know he is in town, right?" Nisha probably could have waited, but asked anyway.

"No. I am not. I know he is here. But I don't know…!"

"Are you planning to meet him?" Nisha asked her before they both placed their orders.

"I don't know, Nisha. I mean I do not see the point in doing so. I am quite sure he is having a gala time out there with his chicks. Besides, he could have also given me a call or something if he wanted us to meet."

"Hmm…okay. Leave all that. You said you wanted to tell me something," Nisha finally asked what she been waiting to.

"Yes. Do not laugh, okay. I am…I actually; well, I registered myself on a matrimony website. That is what I wanted to tell you."

"Okay, there is nothing to laugh at. It is completely normal. So how is that coming along? Any good guys?"

"Not so good, actually. I met a lot of idiots and weird men lately. And the whole 'going there to meet a guy' is kind of freaky. It is not as easy as it sounds. Not cool at all!" Ayesha took a bite of French fries.

"I know that. A couple of my friends have done it too. But trust me, patience is what you need. I know it can get real frustrating at times, but do not give up. You may just meet the right guy. There have to be a few normal people on the website, right?"

"Yes, there have to be," Ayesha was having a tough time trying to deal with the dilemma of whether she should tell Nisha about guy no. 4 or not. But she restrained that thought as she remembered her mother's words, warning her not to tell anyone until anything happened.

"And how is it going with Amit?" Ayesha quickly turned the conversation towards Nisha.

"It is going well. He is a nice guy, he still is. But yes, staying with one's in-laws is a big pain in the ass. It gets on your nerves at times. Believe me; you do not want to do that. Make sure you don't."

"Why, what happened, did they say anything?" Ayesha asked her.

"They don't say anything bad. But you know, no in-laws are cool. All of them expect you one day to start cooking for them, start getting involved in domestic and household duties, more than your office work. They forget the fact that their son hardly does all that, and earns as much as I do, in fact a bit less."

"Hmm…I know. Nothing has really changed. You ever spoke to Amit about it?"

"Yes, a couple of times. But what is the point in dragging him in. He will only get sandwiched in between. It is not his fault."

Ayesha could not disagree with that.

They both finished their sizzlers and left for home.

"Do you want me to call Piyush and make you meet him or something?" Nisha asked the much awaited question of the day.

"Umm…no, don't. But thanks anyway. And keep in touch!" Ayesha had her answer ready as she said goodbye to Nisha.

CHAPTER 14

Guy no. 4 continued…

"Hey! You look good!" Guy no. 4 complimented Ayesha on their second meeting.

"Thanks!" said Ayesha, almost blushing.

"So, let's go and grab something to eat," he said as they moved into the cafe.

Secretly Ayesha had prayed a number of times for this meeting to go well, because finally some guy was able to stand up to her expectations.

"So, how was your day?" Ayesha wanted to initiate the conversation this time.

"Oh, it was good. In fact yesterday there was an article in the city edition of Times of India about my lounge. Even the Zomato guys have given good reviews about it."

"That is nice. Yes, make sure you pay good attention to social media awareness. A lot of people check the reviews of restaurants and bars these days before making a decision to go there," Ayesha showed her genuine concern.

"Thanks for the advice, Ayesha. I certainly will!" Guy no. 4 was quite impressed.

"You tell me, how is your job coming along?" Guy no. 4 asked wondering whether he should ask her to cover his lounge in her newspaper as well. But then he realised, that would make him sound a bit selfish, since it was their second meeting only.

Ayesha carefully took a bite of her cheese grilled sandwich, not letting pieces of bread stick to her lips. She took her time to answer his question as she sipped some coffee from her mug.

"Yes, sorry. My job is good. There are challenges, there are rewards. Overall it is good. I love what I do."

She felt it would have been nice if they could go around for a few months and then see how it went ahead. She was waiting for him to talk about something other than their jobs now. She was waiting for him to talk about them.

"So, what are your parents' views over your getting married? I mean, they must be having expectations of their own right, whether they want you to have a nuclear family or a joint one?" Ayesha asked him, clearly meaning to find out what sort of family system he was looking at.

Guy no. 4 looked a bit perplexed with the question. Maybe he wanted to talk about casual stuff a bit longer. Now he took his time now to answer that question, stirring the coffee once more, although the sugar had already dissolved long back in it.

"Ayesha, there is something I wanted to tell you," he said biting his lower lip.

"Yes, go on," Ayesha asked, wondering whether his parents had some unrealistic expectations.

"It is not about my parents. It is about Kiran."

"Sorry, who?" Ayesha saved the last piece of sandwich to hear his answer first.

"Kiran, my ex-girlfriend. The one I told you about".

"Oh yes, you want to tell me something more. Go on," Ayesha had expected him to share more from his past anyway.

"Well, she called me yesterday. She read the article about my lounge in Times and she said she was really impressed. She…she wants to get back. She hinted that she felt sorry about having broken up with me over a reason like that, and that she had always been thinking about me ever since we stopped talking," he said, looking at Ayesha and waiting for her reaction.

"Oh…okay. And what did you say? Do you want the same?" Ayesha asked him, almost deciding not to eat that last piece of sandwich that she had kept down.

She wanted him to say no. She knew that was not what she would have told anyone to do – to not go back to the love of their life. But she did, maybe a bit selfishly, but she did wait for him to say no.

"Yes, I think I want the same. I'm sorry, Ayesha, I know this is a major screw up on my side. I may have raised your expectations about me and all. But I really love this girl, I always have. And it would be unfair really if I were to hide those feelings from you. I like you. I really do. But it's Kiran. I have been waiting for this day. We both realise that, this lounge was the only reason why we had separated. And now since she is okay with it, I do not see a reason not to go back to her. I am sorry though, I know I wasted a lot of your time," Guy no. 4 spoke at length.

Ayesha tilted her head a bit and gulped some of her words back, down her throat. Her expectations had come crashing down. Maybe she was thinking too much, maybe she had gone a bit too far thinking this could be the final guy, she thought inside.

"Why did you ask me to meet you again today, if you had made up your mind already?" Ayesha asked him with a bit of anger and disappointment.

"I…I could not just tell you over the phone. I felt you are a person who could really understand my situation. And I felt it was best to be discussed out here in person. I really respect you as a person, Ayesha, I do and I always will," Guy no. 4 said.

"Okay!" Ayesha said, realising slowly that her disappointment to hear him say No had nothing to do with him. It was not really his fault.

"I guess you're right in what you are doing," she said.

"Maybe I would have done the same if I were in your place. Good luck to you then!" she said, getting up as she wanted to waste no more time.

"Oh, thanks. Thanks a lot. And once again sorry for wasting your time," Guy no. 4 replied.

"And, yes!" Ayesha said, turning back one last time before she left, "Don't screw it up. Not everyone gets a second chance."

She left the place without waiting for him to answer that. Naveen was waiting outside to pick her up. At least one person would be happy after all.

"Let's go," Ayesha said to Naveen, getting inside the car.

"Are you good?" Naveen could sense the disappointment in her eyes.

"Not really. And yes, let's pick up few cans of beer on our way back."

"But you do not drink beer," Naveen was asking her more questions than she wanted to hear.

"I don't, but I want to today. Can I do something that I want to?"

"Hmm! What happened, Ayesha? It did not go well?" he tried to calm her down.

"Not at all. Remember I told you about this guy's ex-girlfriend? Now he is planning to get back to her. Nothing is wrong with that. But why the hell get me involved in the whole thing? What is my fault? Damn it!" Ayesha tried her best not to cry.

"It's not. It's not your fault. I'm sorry it did not work out," Naveen comforted her and felt sick at wishing secretly that he did wish so.

"So what are you going to do now? I mean you know you can take a break from this matrimony thing for a while, if you want to. Maybe that will be a good thing to do."

"A break? I wish I had to never get into this 'getting married thing'. And sorry, but I do not have 'a while' to wait for things to turn better. I'm just going to have to deal with it. I will have to go ahead with the flow and see whoever the next guy is." Ayesha realised how strong she had become in the past few months as she spoke.

She knew she was not the only one. There are millions of boys and girls out there, trying to find the right person to spend their life with. It doesn't simply fall into place perfectly. She felt sorry for and proud of those not giving up on their search of life partner. It was a vicious cycle that all of them went through – To get ready to meet the new person -> to try and look your best every single time -> to revive your hopes of meeting someone who would fulfil your expectations -> meeting and going through a round of questions and answers repetitively -> to get disappointed or get rejected -> to fall apart -> to get back on your feet and start it all over again.

"I really respect what you're doing, you know. I do. I hope you find your right guy soon," Naveen said as he brought the car to a halt.

"Aww, thank you, Naveen. You are a sweetheart. And you've been so supportive all the time. Sorry I got a bit agitated today. It's just that you know…I had started dreaming all over again. I felt life was coming back to me once more. I was wrong."

"So, are we buying it or what?" Naveen asked her trying to change the topic.

"Buying what?"

"That?" he said pointing to a liquor shop.

"Umm…I don't know. Should we? How high does it get you?" Ayesha finally smiled.

"I don't know. I don't drink," Naveen said like a ten year old boy.

"Oh, god! Naveen, be a man sometimes. Go get two cans. Or you want me to go and get it?"

"What's with being a man? It has nothing to do with that. Besides it is not good to drink, you know," Naveen tried his best to defend himself.

"Are you going or not?" Ayesha said, "I want to try and like a good boy; you're going to try it too,"

"Okay, Miss Ayesha, I give up. I am going. Like a good boy!" Naveen got out of the car to buy some beer for both of them.

They took the car around the hills and parked it at a good spot where they could relish the chilled drops of heaven trapped in those cans.

"I'm just going to have a few sips of it, because I have to drive us back home safely. It is my responsibility," Naveen said, opening the beer can.

"Cheers!" they clashed the beer cans and some beer from each can jumped out.

"Cheers to my fucked up life," Ayesha said without looking at Naveen.

"Hey, come on, it is not that fucked up alright."

"So, you do agree that it is at least a bit?" Ayesha looked at him, sipping the beer as slowly as possible, and continued, "I mean, think about it. How bad can it be – to be single all your life? Lots of people do that. And I kind of get it now, why."

"Are you crazy? You are not going to be. You are too good to be left single," Naveen said what he had always felt.

"Awww, I knew that you were going to say that. You always have been nice to me. And I always well, hey, I'm sorry I never meant to be harsh with your feelings. I guess I have been. Every time you told me that you liked me," Ayesha said, and Naveen could not look straight into her eyes.

Without saying anything for the next few minutes, they passed cold beer down their throat.

"Ayesha?" Naveen broke the gloomy silence and stood in front of her.

"I really like you. I know I'm saying this for the third time in my life to you. But what the hell, who cares? I do like you and you know what, I did always dream of spending the rest of my life with you."

Äyesha looked at his teary eyes that revealed nothing but the truth, and stood frozen like a rock.

"Naveen, I…well!" she did not say anything for a minute.

"Oh my God, Naveen. I actually thought about it, you know. I did. I did just now. What is happening with me? I don't mean you are not good enough for me, but I had never looked at you like that. I did not want to," tears rolled down her cheeks as she said that.

"Hey!" he held her by her shoulders and said, "I am sorry. Maybe I should not have said it at all. You are going through a tough phase and this was probably a really wrong time for me to. But then, I cannot see you having to think of spending your time with some random idiot. You do not have to. You are Ayesha. You deserve so much better. You do!" he did not realise when tears found their way out of his eyes as well.

"You really are a great person, Naveen. Your girlfriend is going to be a real lucky. Trust me on that," she said and they both managed to smile with teary eyes.

"Come here," he held her in his arms and his shoulder was showered with her sorrow.

"You know what sucks, Ayesha? Telling yourself time and time again to believe in something that never really shows up. The problem is not that we all grow up reading and listening to fairy tales. The problem is that some of us actually listen and believe that those are true. I get it, Ayesha. Maybe I'm too nice most of the times. Girls aren't looking for Prince Charming on a white horse. Most would rather go for an asshole in a Mercedes. I get it. Why was I kidding myself?"

"That is not how you think, Naveen, is it?" Ayesha looked at him.

"And yes, most girls go for the bad ones. They do. But they are not the ones who get to choose how you should be. Good or bad, because none of them deserve you. Even if it means narrowing your chances with most, I say you stay as you are. That is what makes you an amazing person. And some girl out there is equally amazing for whom you need to hold onto your belief a little longer," she said, and Naveen smiled back in reply.

"Let's make a deal. One more guy. One more guy you are going to meet like this. And if he is not what you are looking for, we are giving this whole thing a break," he said to her.

"Yes, a break. A break for a long, long time." She agreed and held him tight.

"Naveen held her head with one hand and with the other hand, wiped his own eyes.

"It's okay, we are probably meant to be buddies. And hey, you kept telling me that I'm super sexy, right? So I guess it is not going to be that difficult for me to get a nice girl," he replied.

"Haha, okay. Although I never once said super sexy. I said, you are good looking."

"Hahaha, alright, let's settle for that," he said and they said 'cheers' for the third time.

"Naveen, I think we should get going. Mamma will kill me otherwise." Ayesha spoke with a hairclip between her lips and hands busy tying her hair into a ponytail.

"Yeah, cool, let's go!" Naveen threw the can away immediately, as he wasn't confident of finishing it anyway.

Ayesha pretended to ignore that and got inside the car.

On their way back, they listened to their favourite songs, talked about school time, about Naveen's parents and how long it had been that Ayesha had visited his place to meet them. It was all good. It was short lived. But it was good, nonetheless.

Chapter 15

Good, Bad and Ugly

"Why don't we meet at Royal Cafe this time?" said Guy No. 5 to Ayesha over the phone.

Oh, sorry, let me introduce this guy to you first.

So the guy no. 5 was someone Ayesha decided to meet after a break of a month or two from matrimony websites. She felt she was ready for it. She thought this would be her last attempt.

And the first meeting went well. He was good. Well, not bad, for sure. He wasn't good looking but he was extremely supportive of her career, her dreams and seemed very kind. Actually like a good marriage kind of material, the sort most girls would like to get a hold of.

Ayesha thought she could do away with looks. Looks were not something she considered as her top priority anyway. She just didn't understand why he did not want to meet at her routine coffee place.

"Why not coffee house?" she asked him.

"I think it must have created a lot of negativities about guys you meet or met though the matrimony thing, and I felt maybe, we should try a new place for this meeting," came the clever reply.

"Well, okay if you insist. What time do we meet?"

"Let's meet up at 1pm. Where shall I pick you up from?" he asked like a gentleman.

"Thanks, but my friend will be dropping me off," Ayesha said.

That day, she felt there was something wrong. Or rather something too good to believe in.

What if this was the guy? She wasn't prepared for that. It would mean she would be somebody's wife soon. Not Piyush's. She couldn't look into her own eyes in the mirror. "Am I really ready for it? But screw that thought. Piyush doesn't deserve me either. He hurt my feelings. He did!" The thoughts ran amok in her head as she got ready to meet the guy no. 5.

She knew one thing for sure – she was not going to stretch it beyond this meeting. She believed two meetings are usually more than enough to reject somebody, if not to choose them.

Guy No. 5

Naveen could not drop Ayesha. He was not supposed to anyway, every single time, according to her. It was already very sweet of him to be there every time. She couldn't ask for more.

She took an auto to Royal Cafe and realised she was half an hour behind time. The guy no. 5 had already texted her that he had reached the place.

She paid the auto guy and hurriedly moved upstairs to the restaurant which she had never been to even once. She remembered her mother's words, "Never go to a place you are not familiar with. You never know how these guys are," She hoped her mother was not right this time.

"Hi, I was waiting for you," Guy no. 5 rose from the corner seat of the restaurant and held her hand to help her to her seat.

"Well he's got some confidence!" she thought to herself.

"All good? What made you so late? Traffic is bad, I know," the well rehearsed lines came out of his mouth.

"Yes, sorry about that; my friend couldn't drop me on time."

"That's okay, sweetheart; tell me what will you have? Would you like to have some mocktails to start with?"

"Yes, anything light, I suppose," Aycsha was kind of irritated by his hand touching and his calling her 'sweetheart'.

Guy no. 5 placed the order and waited for a few seconds before getting up from his seat.

"Hey, let me go and confirm whether he has got the order right. Last time the waiter here got me the wrong one," he said, and hurried towards the kitchen.

Ayesha stared into her phone to check the time. 2.30 pm.

Guy no. 5 then returned with the mocktail glasses in his hand.

"Here's your order, Madam!" he said with a smile.

"Thank you!" Ayesha said with a little hesitation, as she took her glass.

"So shall we?" he said raising his glass.

Ayesha did not follow suit. Something told her it was not going right.

"I guess I will eat something first," she said.

"Are you sure? You want to have something else to drink?" he asked, while the waiter appeared with the food he had ordered.

"No, it's okay," Ayesha took a bite of crackling spinach.

They conversed for a while. He talked more about himself this time around. He told her about his family and how much his mother was waiting to meet her. He told her about the farmhouse they owned in south Goa. "It would be lovely to vacation there with you." he suggested to her.

Ayesha did not know for how long they spoke, but she was feeling a bit drowsy now. She looked at the glass. She had not touched it at all. She wondered what was happening. She looked at him. His perfectly ironed shirt and gelled hair, his fake talk and the overly nice image he was portraying! She understood there was something ulterior to it. "Did he do something with the food?" she wondered.

"I need to go to the washroom. I'll be back," she said as she struggled to stand straight.

"Let me help you," Guy no. 5 couldn't stifle the smile and put his arm around her.

"I can go by myself!" Ayesha was too weak to resist his advances.

"It's okay, sweetie. You'll be fine," his hand moved from her shoulder to her waist.

It was followed by a tap on his shoulder.

"SHE SAID SHE DOESN'T NEED YOUR HELP!"

Guy no. 5 looked puzzled at a six feet guy standing tall in front of him.

"Who…?"

A punch was aimed straight at his nose before he could complete the sentence and he was knocked down to the ground.

Piyush

"Piyush? What are you…how are you? How did you know I'm here?"

"Later. First, let's get out of this place."

Ayesha smiled her perfect smile in reply to his voice and he helped her move out of the restaurant she pledged never to visit again in life.

"Are you alright? Drink more of that lemonade. Will make you feel better," Piyush looked at her while he steered his car though the early evening traffic.

"Yes, I'm good now. Thank you so much. I don't know what happened. I was really scared. I feel stupid to even go and meet a guy like him."

"Not your fault. There are lot of such con men on Matrimony these days. They spike drinks and what not. You should be careful, Ayesha," he spoke to her in a fatherly tone.

"How did you know I was meeting people from Matrimony?"

"I got in touch with Naveen recently. He told when I asked about you," Piyush said, without looking at her.

"Oh. Naveen never told me."

"That is because I asked him not to. But then today he texted me saying he was not able to drop you, and that you were planning to go to this weird restaurant to meet this guy. I did not know whether I have any right to call you or what to do. I just came here to…well, I just came here! It was spontaneous actually!" Piyush smiled nervously as he managed to explain.

"It was sweet, nevertheless, Piyush. Thank you so much!" Ayesha said, and at the same time, disliked the formality that had appeared between them.

They stopped at Polka Dots. It was Piyush's favourite Italian restaurant. He simply loved the lasagne they cooked there. She shared some today with him, like old times. Piyush made sure there were fewer things that would spark memories from the past and Ayesha tried just the opposite. Over the course of their conversation, she realised that Piyush had been far stronger when it came to hiding anything that was left over in his heart for her. He had moved on. Farther than she could have ever had. But then he was the same guy she had fallen for, and she was the same girl he had been in love with. Only the sands of time had betrayed them. Time had killed the moment they were sharing now.

"So have you ever thought about getting back, you know?" she finally dared to ask.

"A thousand times! But then we both know it is not wise," Piyush replied immediately.

"What do you mean? Not wise?"

"Ayesha, we separated for a reason. Reasons, in fact! Yes, there were sleepless nights that I spent thinking that one day I would just land at your door step with flowers in my hand. And I knew I could take you back. I knew we would be very happy to see each other. But then there are mornings after that. Mornings when I will wake up as the person I am, and you too. Waking up as what we are today, with things that we don't like about each other. I had issues with you and you disliked several things about me. And let's be honest, those things are still very much there. Those things have not changed. We still are the same people. It would be unfair to the past two years of trying to get over each other. That wasn't easy for either of us. But we are moving on, aren't we? So, I think we should keep looking ahead."

"You are trying to say we are not compatible, and yet, we were in love for, like, four years?" Ayesha did not fall for his words this time.

"All I'm trying to say, Ayesha, is that we were 24, 25 year olds when we met. We had not seen even 25 percent of our lives and maybe this is how it was supposed to be. I'm glad that I spent that beautiful time together with you, but I guess that was it. Maybe it wasn't meant to last forever."

"Hmm…I guess you are right, Piyush. And anyway, I'm happy that it did not work out. Because you should know, you snore like crazy when you sleep," Ayesha laughed as she said that.

"What?? I do not snore!"

"Yes, you do, Piyush. And also, you are a cat person!" she mocked him.

"So what, being a cat person isn't that bad, is it?" And Ayesha, let me tell you, you suck at Karaoke nights. You scream when you sing. People were clapping that night because they were getting entertained."

"Hahaha!" they both kept laughing and Ayesha felt there was no more anger left in her heart. They had just helped each other burn the bridges together.

"Hey, I'm sorry though. I mean about Kim's thing. That shouldn't have…!" Piyush finally apologized to her in person.

"Well, doesn't matter now, Piyush. It does not. Anyway, are you like dating her or something now?"

"No no, I never dated her. She has gone to London now," he replied. "Ayesha I'm too unstable right now. My job, this continuous travelling, poetry in between; I don't know where I will be tomorrow. You understand me right?"

"Hmm…I do."

"Besides I think you deserve a great guy. You still look so beautiful. You should be with someone like Naveen. 'Someone like', because I know you never looked at him that way. Just try and be patient for a little more time. And stop with the matrimony thing for a while. It is great. But it doesn't work well for everyone. I don't think it is meant for you."

"Hmm. I will think over it, Piyush. Thanks. Anyway, I think we should leave. It is time," Ayesha said and they got up feeling a bit happy, a bit sad. He dropped her near her house. Standing at the edge of their goodbyes, they lost track of words and chose to speak with their eyes instead. They did not hug each other goodbye. For their hearts were too weak to let go of each other.

Ayesha turned around to watch his car move out of her apartment. Maybe he was watching the rear-view mirror for her to look behind. Maybe. She would never find out.

Chapter 16

Nights are not the same every day. Some nights are longer than the others. Especially when you are lonesome! And tonight Ayesha was lonesome. She wanted to pinch herself several times that she had actually met Piyush after such a long time. She couldn't decide if it was good or bad. Every time she played it in her head, she paused upon the good parts. Him throwing a punch at Guy no. 5, taking care of her later, his jokes, his smile, him being sorry for what had happened. She kept rewinding the cassette in her head for fear of losing track of it.

She started typing a text to Naveen. She told him how her day went and repeated how she had not thought of meeting Piyush today even in her dreams. Naveen's reply to that text wasn't very quick. He told her that she needed to calm down, and probably take a break from the whole matrimony thing. They decided to meet up next day, on one condition that they were not going to talk about marriage at all.

Ayesha had slept late that night, and in the morning, the sun bestowed no courtesy on her sleepy eyes. Her alarm clock sang for the second time and she put it on the snooze mode again. With a face half shoved inside the pillow, she looked at the sunlit window pane. It looked like a brighter day today. The day seemed fresh, although she had had hardly any sleep last night. She looked at her office bag, then outside the window, and finally at the clock. The decision came easily.

"Mom! I'm not going to office today. Don't prepare lunch for me. I'll be going out with Naveen," Ayesha's voice echoed from inside the washroom and managed to reach her mother's ears.

Ayesha felt it was a good lesson. Every guy she met so far, including Piyush, had all taught her something. It was time to look ahead. Life wasn't so bad after all. She was lost in her world of thoughts as water drops from the shower kissed her face and jumped off her shoulders to the floor. She always did find comfort in a long shower. It was peaceful despite the sound of gushing water. It gave her time for herself and calmed her heartbeats down.

She moved the wet hair sticking to her face behind her ears and turned the shower knob off. Standing in front of the bathroom mirror, she stared at her reflection.

"*You still look beautiful!*" Piyush's words whispered in her ears, and she smiled at the thought.

She took time that day to get ready, unlike every day. She combed her hair neatly, put on mascara, tried a couple of clothes and wore her newly bought ballet shoes. Kissing her mother goodbye, she stepped outside. Naveen was waiting for her.

"Oh my god, not bad at all, Naveen! See, I told you it will look good on you," she admired the shirt they had bought together a week earlier.

"Thanks, and you are also looking good" he said, as he watched her smile.

Chapter 17

At Western Coffee Place

"You know Naveen, I still find it funny that you did not have the guts to ask Pooja out, back in college."

"Oh, c'mon, stop teasing me about that now, will you? It has been years to that episode." Naveen took a sip of coffee.

"But you did like her a lot, right? I mean, you could've got in touch with her again. What are you so afraid of? Asking someone out isn't that difficult, is it?" Ayesha was really concerned about him.

"Let us just stop talking about it, please!" Naveen said, and went into silence for a minute.

"Ayesha, I would rather want to know today why you never liked me?" he said, gathering confidence.

"Ughhh, Naveen, we spoke about this. Let us not go there again."

"No, but I want to. I asked you out three times so far, and each time you said no. That kind of kicked my pride in smithereens. I know maybe Pooja, or some girl, will say 'Yes' to me someday. But I am afraid now. I am afraid that 'No' is also a possibility. I just want to know if I lack something. What is it that you did not see in me? If you don't tell me, then probably, I might just keep repeating that mistake," Naveen spoke his heart out.

"There is nothing wrong with you. You are right. You always were. It was just me that you were not right about, Naveen. And I consider myself lucky to have you in my life. Not every girl gets a best friend as good as you are. I mean it. And to tell you…!" Ayesha paused, before continuing,

"Naveen, you might want to take a look behind!"

"What happened?" he said, turning around to spot a girl from their college sitting across the table and looking at them. Pooja!

"Wow, what a coincidence! What do I do? You think she saw me looking at her? Should I go and speak to her? Will you come along? Do I…?"

"Naveen, just stop panicking. It's Pooja. And yes, it's a lovely coincidence. Now be a man and go and talk to her. Share your feelings. There won't come a better time." Ayesha patted his shoulder and made him go.

She smiled as she watched him going over to Pooja's table and taking a seat there. She hoped that something would work out between them. She got a good feeling out of it.

But soon her thoughts shifted focus from Naveen and Pooja to her own life. She thought about herself. It was the first time Ayesha was sitting alone at that table at her favourite coffee house. The same place where she had met five guys through matrimony websites. She looked at Naveen and Pooja again and tried to guess what they were talking about. She hoped it was not about Chemistry notes this time.

"Madam, here is your sizzling brownie!" the waiter placed the coffee and brownie in front of her.

"But I did not ask for one," she said, waking up from her thoughts.

"Yes, Mam, it is on the house," he replied, and walked away with an empty tray.

Ayesha looked in the direction of the kitchen in surprise.

And she was greeted with a smile she had seen before. A long time ago, in fact. A guy with a dusky complexion, wearing a waist coat walked slowly towards her table. The same guy she had mistaken for Guy no. 1. The only guy she had found charming at this cafe so far. While she watched him walk in style, she now recalled all the times she had seen him here. She remembered how he always appeared with a bill or cheque every time her meeting with the matrimony guys went on for too long. She also remembered seeing him somewhere other than at this coffee place. She was having a hard time trying to recall where.

"Hi!" He came to her table.

"Hi, I…I don't understand," Ayesha couldn't come up with a perfect reply.

"Let me help you with that," he said in his husky voice, and took a seat in front of her.

"My name is…!"

Guy No. 6

"I am looking after this cafe. As in, I started this cafe around four years back. So I know who my regular customers are," he said, smiling.

"That still doesn't explain much," Ayesha replied, playing with her hair.

"I know. Allow me!" He said, pushing the sleeves of his white shirt further up.

"Well, I always saw you coming here to meet guys for probably marriage or something. Sorry, none of my business, I know. But I couldn't help. Some of them were really weird," he said and Ayesha couldn't control her laughter.

"Yes, they were. Go on!" she said, looking at his dark brown eyes.

"So I used to see you with them and do a math in my head as to how soon you are going to reject that particular guy! And trust me, I was usually spot on. In fact sometimes, when I felt that you were getting way too bored by a particular guy, I would come there with a cheque asking you two to clear the table. I'm sure you hated me for that. But believe me, I had only good intentions. I liked you and wanted you to get rid of those stupid guys," he spoke at length.

"You what?" Ayesha stopped eating the vanilla ice cream.

"I liked you. I mean I like you. I said that right, I did. And that is why I'm sitting here right now," Guy no. 6 replied and continued,

"Ayesha, I don't think you remember that well. But I do. We were in the same college. Not for long. But we were. I had come on tour to your college. I was in Piyush's batch, if that helps you recall it," he said. Ayesha suddenly had a spark of memory in her head. She now remembered seeing him with Piyush at their college canteen.

"Oh, I'm sorry; I did not remember the first time," she apologized.

"You do not need to. Not your fault. I know about Piyush and you. In fact, I knew Piyush quite well. He would always speak about you. But the point being, I always had a crush over you back then. And then, you came to my cafe the other day. I felt I should just come and speak with you. But of course, the guy who had come to visit did that first, and all I was left with was to take an order," he said with mock innocence.

"Wow! I cannot believe all this happened. I mean, it is kind of sweet of you. I cannot say I like you, because we have hardly spoken," Ayesha blushed as she said that.

"I know. But I really really like you. I do. And I hope you spend some time of your busy schedule with me. Because Miss Ayesha, I really want to be with you, and I hope someday, you decide to spend the rest of your smiles with me."

Ayesha smiled. It was one of the best proposals she had ever had, and by one of the best looking men she had come across.

"You indeed are the cutest random guy to walk up to me and say that," she said, and they smiled together.

"Care for a little walk outside?" he asked.

"Umm…sure!" Ayesha said, turning to see Naveen and Pooja sharing a coffee and giggling.

She knew at that moment that life was good.

So after the long walk,
several phone
conversations and the
dates that followed...

Ayesha and Guy no. 6 were strolling around her apartment.

"So, tell me what do you do when you are not working at your coffee place? I mean, obviously you've got people working for you there," Ayesha asked him.

"Well, mostly I go and work for 'Paws'," he replied.

"Paws?"

"Yes. It's a community that works towards the welfare of animals."

"Of course I know what it is. So you are saying that you are a Cat person?" she said.

"Nope. A Dog person! Why would you ask that?" Guy no. 6 said.

"Nothing. Just like that!" Ayesha exclaimed, and reaffirmed the fact that she had, in fact, found the right guy.

And he knew only too well how much she liked dogs.

"By the way, I read your article on the hapless state of stray dogs in Deccan Chronicle. It was a good read. You write really well."

"Thank you!" Ayesha smiled, and continued, "I was a content writer back then, when I wrote that piece." She lifted her shoulders up as she said that.

"So you must have met a lot of people for this marriage thing, right?" Guy no. 6 asked her.

"Well, yes, six in total, actually…so far!"

"Wow, crazy it must have been!" he said and held open an umbrella to cover them both from the little drizzle that had just begun.

"So, was it good, bad, how was it? Sorry, I keep going to that topic."

"It was fine. Just like they say in fairy tales – "You have to kiss six frogs before you meet your prince," Ayesha said, looking deep into his eyes.

"Hmm! Yeah, I've heard that! Hold on! You said I was the sixth one, right? Or the seventh one? That means I…?" he said, as Ayesha held on to his hand.

They laughed and the raindrops rhythmically tap danced around their feet.

Watching them walk hand in hand, Cupid chuckled, sitting on a cloud no. 9. He was happy that there still lived people who believed that he was doing his job just fine. A trifle late sometimes, but nevertheless doing it right.